THE MYSTERY THAT NEVER WAS

D1048501

This Armada book belongs to:

_____

_____

_____

Enid Blyton

THE MYSTERY
THAT NEVER WAS

Armada

First published in the U.K. in this edition in 1976 by
William Collins Sons & Co. Ltd., London and Glasgow.
First published in Armada in 1983 by
Fontana Paperbacks,
8 Grafton Street, London W1X 3LA.

This impression 1984

Printed and bound in Great Britain by
William Collins Sons & Co. Ltd, Glasgow

CONTENTS

CHAPTER 1

NEWS AT BREAKFAST-TIME

NICKY FRASER came down the stairs at top speed, his dog Punch at his heels barking in excitement. The little terrier flung himself against the dining-room door and it flew open, crashing against the wall.

The family were at breakfast. Nicky's father gave a roar of anger. " NICKY ! What's the matter with you this morning ? Take that dog out of the room ! "

Mrs. Fraser put down the coffee-jug and fended off Punch who was leaping up joyfully at her. Grandma smiled at Nicky, and tapped his father on the hand.

" *Just* like you used to be when you were his age ! " she said.

" Hallo, family ! " said Nicky, beaming round as he went to the sideboard to help himself to scrambled eggs. " I can see you've forgotten what day this is ! "

" I told you to take that dog out of the room," said his father.

7

" Day ? Well, what particular day *is* it ? " said Grandma. " Not a birthday—that I do know ! "

" No, Granny ! It's the first day of the hols ! Ha—four glorious long weeks to do just what I like in ! " He began to sing loudly. " Hey derry, hey derry ho, hey . . ."

" Stop that row," said his father. " And take that . . ."

" Dog out of the room ! " finished Nicky. He put his plate down on the table and turned to give his father a sudden hug. " Oh, Dad—it's the first day of the hols. Come on, Dad—I bet *you* used to sing for joy, too ! "

" Sit down," said his father. " *I'll* sing for joy —I hope—when I see your report. Punch, get off my feet."

Punch removed himself and went to sit on Grandma's feet. He gave her leg a loving lick. He loved her very much. She *never* shouted at him !

" I suppose you and Kenneth have plenty of plans for these holidays ? " said the old lady. " It's lucky he lives next door."

" Jolly lucky ! " said Nicky, buttering his toast. " Actually we haven't any *definite* plans. We thought we'd teach Punch a few more tricks— like fetching shoes or slippers for people. Granny, wouldn't you be pleased if Punch fetched you your slippers to put on, when you came in from a walk ? "

" Good heavens ! " said his father. " Don't tell me we're going to find slippers strewn about all over the place ! "

" What's that dog eating ? " said Mrs. Fraser, as a loud crunching noise came from under the table. " Oh *Nicky*—you've given him a piece of toast again."

" I bet it was Grandma who gave it to him," said Nicky. " Punch, stop eating so rudely. Dad —are you going to give me my usual ten shillings if my report's good ? And a pound if it's super ? "

" Yes, yes, yes," said his father. " Now be quiet. I want to read the paper, and your mother hasn't even read her letters yet."

Mrs. Fraser was reading a short letter. Nicky's sharp eyes recognised the handwriting.

" I bet that's from Uncle Bob ! " he said. " Isn't it, Mother ? Has he had any exciting jobs lately ? "

" Yes—it *is* from my brother Bob," said his mother, putting down the letter. " He's coming to stay with us for a while, and . . ."

" CHEERS ! " cried Nicky, putting his cup down with a thump. " Did you hear that, Punch ? "

Punch barked joyfully, and came out from under the table, his tail thumping against Mr. Fraser's leg. He was promptly pushed back again.

" Mother ! I say, Mother, he isn't coming down here on a *job*, is he ? " asked Nicky, his eyes shining.

" I bet he is ! Mother, will he do some sleuthing here ? I'll help him, if so. So will Ken. What's the job ? Is it something we . . . ? "

" Nicky ! Don't get so excited ! " said his mother. " No. Uncle Bob is coming down here because he's been ill and wants a rest."

" Oh, blow ! I thought he might be hunting a murderer or a swindler or a—a kidnapper or something," said Nicky, disappointed. " You know, Mother, I'm the only boy at school whose uncle is a detective ! "

" A private investigator," his mother corrected him. " His work is . . ."

" Oooh, I know all about his *work*," said Nicky, taking another piece of toast. " They've got plenty of investigators on television. Last week one had a frightfully difficult case to solve. It ended up in an aeroplane chase, and . . ."

" You watch television too much," said his father, gathering up his letters. " And now listen to me— if your Uncle Bob is coming here for a rest, he will NOT want hordes of gaping schoolboys coming here to listen to his adventures ! Bob is not supposed to talk about them, anyway—they are private. Nobody is to be told that he's the uncle you've been boasting about."

" Oh Dad—can't I even tell *Ken* ? " said Nicky, in dismay.

" Well, I suppose you can't *possibly* keep any-thing from Kenneth," said his father, going out of the room. " But ONLY Kenneth, mind ! "

" I shall tell him immediately after breakfast ! " said Nicky, passing another bit of toast under the table. " Did you hear the news, Punch ? Whoops —we'll have some fun with Uncle Bob. Mother, have you ever seen him in any of his disguises ? Can I telephone him and ask him to come in dis-guise to-morrow, to see if Ken and I can spot him ? "

" Oh don't be so ridiculous, Nicky," said his mother. " And listen—there's to be no going over to Ken's until you have tidied up your room. All your school books seem to be spread over the floor ! "

" Right, Mother ! " said Nicky. " Gosh, to think it's only the *first* day of the hols ! Come on, Punch ! You're going to be busy the next few weeks, learning a whole lot of new tricks ! That's the time to learn, you know—when you're young ! And you're hardly a year old yet. Scram ! "

Punch scrammed. He shot out into the hall, sending the mat flying, and up the stairs, barking. He thought it must be a Saturday as Nicky was not going to school. He raced into Nicky's room and raced round and round the bed at top speed, barking madly. Oh what joy to have Nicky all day long !

Nicky picked up all his scattered books, and de-

cided to stack them in the fireplace, out of the way.
" All my bookshelves are full," he told Punch.
" So the fireplace is the obvious place. They'll go
half-way up the chimney, I expect. Then I'll slip

downstairs and phone Uncle Bob. Shut up barking
now, Punch—you'll have Mother shouting up to
us."

He slipped downstairs to the study after his bout
of tidying. No one seemed to be about. He went
in, shut the door and sat down by the telephone.

He rang his uncle's number and waited impatiently, Punch sitting as close to him as possible.

His uncle's secretary answered. " Oh, is that you, Mr. Hewitt ? " said Nicky. " Well, listen. Uncle Bob's coming to stay with us to-morrow. Tell him I'll meet him with my friend Kenneth —and we'd like him to come in disguise just to see if we can spot him. You won't forget, will you ? "

" I'll tell him," said the voice at the other end of the phone. " That's if I see him before he leaves but it may be that I . . ."

Nicky heard footsteps approaching along the hall, said good-bye hurriedly, and put down the receiver. He couldn't help feeling that his father would consider it a waste of the telephone to ask Uncle Bob such a thing. Luckily the footsteps passed the study door, and Nicky crept out unseen.

" Come on, Punch ! We'll go and find Ken and tell him Uncle Bob's coming ! " he said to the excited dog. " Race you out into the garden—GO ! "

CHAPTER 2

DOWN IN THE SHED

PUNCH took the short-cut that the boys always used
—out of the back door, through the yard, down the
garden to the hole in the hedge. Mrs. Hawes, the
woman who came in to help each day, shook her
broom at Punch as he flew past, almost tripping
her up.

"You and that boy!" she said. "Sixty miles
an hour and no brakes! Give me a cat any time!"

Punch and Nicky squeezed through the hole in

the yew hedge, and Nicky gave a piercing whistle. It was immediately answered by Kenneth, who was down in his garden shed. Punch arrived there before Nicky, and flung himself on Kenneth, whom, next to Nicky, he adored with all his heart. He licked him from top to toe, giving little whines all the time.

"You'll wear your tongue out, Punch," said Kenneth. "Stop it now. I've already washed twice this morning. What a dog! Hallo, Nicky! I see Punch is his usual fat-headed self. Hope you are too!"

Nicky grinned. "Hallo, Ken! I say, isn't it grand, no school this morning! First thing I thought of when I woke. How are your guinea-pigs?"

"Fine. I've just finished feeding them," said Ken. "Look at this tiddler—the youngest of the lot, and the cutest. Get down, Punch. He's an awfully *nosy* dog, isn't he, Nicky? Nosy would be a much better name for him than Punch."

"Listen, Ken—I've a bit of news," said Nicky, pulling Punch away from the guinea-pig cage. "Wait a minute though—where's that nosy sister of yours? She's not anywhere about, is she?"

"She might be," said Ken, cautiously, and went to the door of the shed to see if his sister

Penelope was in sight. " No—all clear," he said, and came back.

" Penny's just about as nosy as old Punch here," said Nicky. " Listen, Ken—you know my Uncle Bob—the one who's a sort of detective ? "

" Yes. What about him ? Has he solved some mystery or other ? " said Ken, interested at once. " I say, did you see that detective play on TV last night—where nobody could make out who stole the . . . ? "

" No, I didn't. Do listen, Ken. Uncle Bob is coming this morning—and I phoned him and asked him to come in disguise, so that we could show him how good we are at tracking people and seeing through any disguise. Uncle Bob's a wow at disguising himself—he showed me his Special Wardrobe once—bung full of all kinds of different clothes—and hats ! You should have seen them ! "

" Gosh ! " said Ken. " I say—do you think he's come down to do a spot of detective work here in our town ? Can we help him ? We're pretty good at disguises ourselves, aren't we ? Do you remember that time when you dressed up as a guy and I wheeled you down-town on Guy Fawkes Day ? If you hadn't had a coughing fit nobody would ever have seen through *that* disguise ! "

" My mother says he hasn't come to do any sleuthing here," said Nicky, mournfully. " But, of course, he might *not* have told her, if anything was up. He's supposed to be coming because he needs a rest."

"*That's* a likely story, I *don't* think!" said Ken, scornfully. "I never in my life saw anyone so bursting with health as your Uncle Bob. The way he made us walk for miles, too—do you remember? Personally I'm quite glad to hear he needs a rest!"

"Well, anyway, he's coming to-day," said Nicky. "And, as I said, I asked if he'd come in disguise. He's always one for a game, you know —so what disguise do you think he'll wear?"

There was a pause. Ken scratched his head. "Well—he might dress up as an old man," he said.

"Yes, he might," said Nicky. "Or as a postman. I saw a postman's uniform in his wardrobe. Anyway, there's one thing he *can't* disguise, and that's his big feet!"

"Would he disguise himself as a *woman*?" asked Ken.

"I don't *think* so—the voice would be difficult," said Nicky, considering the matter. "And the walk, too. Uncle Bob's got a proper man's walk."

"Well, so has Penny's riding mistress," pointed out Ken. "And her voice is jolly deep. Like this!" And to Punch's alarmed surprise he suddenly spoke in a curious, deep-down, hoarse voice. Punch growled at once.

" It's all right, Punch," grinned Nicky, patting him. " That was a jolly good effort, Ken. Well, what we'll do is this—go to the station and meet the London train with old Punch here, and . . ."

" But that wouldn't be fair," objected Ken. " Punch would recognise him at once by his smell. We'd better leave him behind. He'd do what he always does when he sees or smells anyone he knows—go round them in circles, barking his head off."

" Yes, you're right. We won't take old Punch then," said Nicky. " He'll be awfully upset, though. We'll lock him in your shed."

" No. He'll howl the place down," said Ken. " Lock him in *yours*."

" Right," said Nicky. " Do you hear that, Punch, old thing ? In the shed for you, see, while we go walky-walkies—and if you don't make a sound, I'll give you a great big bone."

" Wuff ! " said Punch, wagging his tail violently at the word " bone." The boys patted him, and he rolled over on his back, doing his favourite bicycling act with all four legs in the air.

" Ass," said Nicky. " What shall we do till midday, Ken ? The London train comes in about five past twelve."

" Sh ! " said Ken, as the sound of someone singing came on the air. " There's Penny. Pretend to be tidying up the shed in case she wants us to do anything."

At once the two boys began to pull boxes about feverishly, and straighten up things on the dirty shelves. A face peered in at the door.

" Oh, so there you are," said Penny, and came right into the shed. " *You've* been a long time feeding your guinea-pigs, Ken ! Mother wondered what you were up to."

" You mean *you* did ! " said Ken, busily brushing a great deal of dust off a shelf, all over Penny. " Look out ! We're busy, as you can see. Like to help—though it's a pretty dirty job, cleaning out this shed."

" *Well !* I've never seen you clean out this shed before ! " said Penny, sneezing as the dust flew around. " I wondered if you'd like to mend my bicycle-brake for me. It's gone again."

" Penny—we're BUSY ! " said Ken. " I'll do it to-night. Or you can ask Gardener. He's good at bikes."

" Well, I certainly don't want to stay here in *this* mess and muddle ! " said Penny. " Get down, Punch. *Now* look how he's dirtied me with his paws ! "

" Oh, for goodness' sake, go away," said Ken,

and swished another cloud of dust from a nearby shelf. Penny sneezed and hurried out. Nicky looked at Ken.

" Shall *I* go and mend her brake ? " he said. " She just *might* have an accident, you know. We've plenty of time."

" I can hear her asking Gardener," said Ken, climbing down from the box he was standing on. " She's a Nosy Parker—only came down to see what we were doing ! Why *are* girls so nosy ? You're lucky not to have a sister."

" Oh, I wouldn't mind a *little* one," said Nicky. " It's not much fun being an ' only,' you know. It's a lucky thing for me that you live next door. Still —I've got old Punch ! "

" Wuff ! " said Punch, and licked his hand. Ken looked round the shed. " We might as well clean it up properly now," he said. " We've nothing to do till midday, when the London train comes in. Shan't we get filthy ! "

They worked hard, and quite enjoyed themselves. " My word—we're a sight !" said Nicky. " I'd better go in and change—and hope I shan't bump into Mother on the way ! Meet you outside my gate in a quarter of an hour—and then we'll just show Uncle Bob that we can see through *any* disguise he's put on ! Come on, Punch—you've got to be locked up, old fellow, till we come back ! "

CHAPTER 3

WHICH IS UNCLE BOB?

THE TWO BOYS left a very angry Punch locked up in Nicky's shed. "Hope Penny won't hear him howling and let him out," said Ken. "I say, I'd better come in with you while you put on something clean, and give myself a brush. I'm pretty filthy too—but if I go into my own house and Mum sees me I might be sent on all kinds of errands."

"Well, come on in, then," said Nicky. "Back way, then we'll only see Mrs. Hawes, our daily woman."

Mrs. Hawes stared at them in surprise, as they tiptoed through the kitchen. "Well, there now— I never knew the Missis had ordered two sweeps for the chimneys this morning!" she said, as they went by her, grinning cheekily.

Nicky put on a clean sweater and washed his face, while Ken brushed himself vigorously, sending black clouds of dust all over the bedroom. Through the open window came woeful howls from the garden shed. Poor Punch!

"Now to slip out without Mother seeing me,"

said Nicky. " I don't want to have to stop and do odd jobs just as we're off to meet the train."

They crept down the stairs and made for the kitchen again. An astonished voice called after them. " Oh! *There* you are, Nicky! Where have you been all morning? I wanted you to . . ."

" Sorry, Mother—we're off to meet the London train! " shouted Nicky. " Uncle Bob, you know! "

" Yes, but wait, Nicky, you silly boy, you won't be . . ." began his mother, coming out of the sitting-room after them. But the boys had disappeared, and the kitchen door banged.

" Narrow escape! " panted Nicky, racing round to the front gate. " Come on! We'll just get to the station in time."

The train was signalled as they ran on to the platform. " Now you keep a watch on the people coming from the back of the train, and I'll watch the front," said Nicky. " And remember to look for BIG FEET! "

Ken remembered quite well what Nicky's Uncle Bob looked like—an upstanding fellow with keen eyes, determined mouth, and clean-shaven.

" Still, he might wear a false moustache or a beard this morning," thought Ken. " And stand bent over like an old man." He stood waiting as the train came in by him and pulled to a stop.

Six people stepped down from the carriages.

Two were women, both small. They could be ruled out at once. One was a boy, who went whistling down the platform. That left three. Nicky and Ken looked at them closely.

An oldish man with a beard—shuffling along, head bent forward—glasses on his nose—and large feet! Nicky brightened at once. " Might quite well be Uncle Bob! " he thought, and fell in behind him at once.

Of the other two, one was a postman with a large bag. He too had large feet, and was bent under the weight of his heavy bag. He had a small moustache, and mopped his face with a handker- chief as he went, giving a large sneeze as he passed the boys. They nudged one another.

" Bet that's him! " whispered Ken. " You fol- low him and I'll follow the old chap—just in case ! I don't think that other person's any good. Small feet ! "

Nicky nodded. He followed close behind the postman, wishing he could get a better look at his face. Gosh—he certainly had large feet! Nicky tried to peer into his face as he walked past him, but the man was still mopping his nose. He slung his bag from one shoulder to the other, and it knocked against Nicky.

" Hey ! " said Nicky, almost bowled over by the weight of the bag. " Got a cold, Uncle Bob ? "

"What you following me about for?" growled the postman. "Think you're being funny calling me your uncle? Clear off!"

His voice was not deep, but rather hoarse as if he had a bad cold. Nicky decided that it was decidedly a false voice. He gave the postman a nudge with his arm. "Come on, Uncle Bob! Own up! I'd know your voice anywhere, even though you're making it as croaky as an old crow's. But it's a jolly good disguise!"

The postman put his bag down with a thump and glared at Nicky. "Now if I have any more funny business from *you*, me lad, I'll talk to that policeman over there, see?"

The postman was now staring straight at Nicky, and he could see the man's whole face very clearly —good gracious, it was nothing like his Uncle Bob's face—and the little moustache was certainly real! Nicky began to feel most uncomfortable.

"Sorry!" he said, awkwardly. "I just thought you were—er—in disguise, you know. I was looking for someone else!"

"Now you clear off, see? And if my voice sounds like an old crow's, so would yours with a cold like mine," said the angry postman, and sneezed again so violently that his postman's cap almost flew off.

"It was a mistake," said poor Nicky, red in the

" Come on, Uncle Bob! Own up! "

face. " I apologise ! " And he raced off after Ken, who was still following the old man. Ken was lucky, thought Nicky—*that* must be Uncle Bob, shuffling along, pulling at his beard and mumbling to himself.

He caught up with Ken and raised his eyebrows, muttering, " Any luck ? "

Ken nodded. " I think so. Haven't said anything, yet, though. Look at his feet ! "

Nicky looked. Yes—they were just about the same size as Uncle Bob's—and so were his hands. That beard was clever—hid half the face ! The old man suddenly stopped, pulled out a cigarette case and lit a cigarette, holding the match with trembling fingers. He flipped the match away with finger and thumb. " Just like Uncle Bob always does ! " thought Nicky. " Aha, Uncle Bob ! I'll have a little fun with you ! "

So he fell into step beside the old man and began to talk. " Do you know the way to Mr. Fraser's house ? " he asked, and Ken gave a grin, for that, of course was Nicky's home. " I'll take you there myself, if you like."

" Don't play the fool," grunted the old man in a husky voice. " What are you two boys following me for ? "

" What big feet you've got, Uncle Bob ! " said Nicky. " And do let me feel your nice thick beard !"

The old man looked angry and a little frightened. He walked on, saying nothing, then suddenly crossed the road to where the town policeman stood, stolid and burly.

"Constable, will you take these boys' names, and tell their fathers they have been molesting me?" said the old man. The policeman stared in astonishment at Nicky and Ken, whom he knew well.

"Now what have you two been doing to old Mr. Holdsworth?" he demanded. Then he turned back to the old man. "All right, sir," he said. "I'll deal with this for you. Young rascals!"

"I say, Constable—is he *really* an old man?" said Nicky, taken aback, as he watched the old fellow go off, mumbling. "I thought he was my Uncle Bob in disguise. Is he *really* a Mr. Holdsworth?"

"Now look here, Nicky Fraser, *you* know he's an old man all right, and no more your Uncle Bob than *I* am!" said the policeman. "Don't you start getting into trouble like some of the youngsters in this town! Playing the fool and making fun of old people isn't the sort of thing your parents would like to hear about."

"It was a mistake, really it was," stammered poor Nicky, and Ken nodded his head too, scared. "You see . . ."

"Go home," said the policeman, impatiently.

" I've no time to waste on silly kids that don't act their age. *Next* time I'll deal with you properly."

He marched out into the road, and began sorting out a small traffic jam. The two boys, red in the face, hurried home. They felt very foolish indeed.

Nicky saw his mother in the front garden and yelled to her. " Mother! We went to meet Uncle Bob, and he and wasn't on the train."

" Well, no wonder! " said his mother. " Didn't you hear what I called out to you, when you left in such a hurry? I said he was coming by *car*! "

" BLOW! " said both boys at once. Nicky groaned. " Gosh—what asses we've been! What time *is* Uncle Bob arriving, then? "

At that very moment a sports car drew up in front of the house, and the horn was blown loudly. The boys swung round.

" It's Uncle Bob! Goodness, Uncle Bob, we've been meeting several of you at the station! What a smashing car! Come on in, you're just in time for dinner! "

CHAPTER 4

GOOD OLD UNCLE BOB !

UNCLE BOB was just the same as ever, except that he was a bit thinner, and rather pale. Nicky's mother, his sister, made a fuss of him.

" Oh Bob, dear ! Whatever have you been doing to yourself ? You've gone as thin as a rake ! "

" Now Lucy, don't exaggerate ! " said Uncle Bob, and gave her such a bear-hug that she gasped. " I'm a bit overdone, that's all ! If you can put up with me for a week or two I'll soon be as fit as a fiddle ! Hallo, boys—what's this about meeting several of me at the station ? "

The boys told him, and he roared with laughter. " You're a couple of idiots ! I can see you need a few lessons in detective work ! Come on in and help me to unpack my bag."

It was grand to have Uncle Bob staying with them again. Punch was thrilled too. When the boys let him out of the shed, giving him a bone as they had promised, he ignored the bone completely, and tore up the garden, barking loudly. He had already heard Uncle Bob's voice, and not even a

juicy bone could tempt him! He flung himself on
Uncle Bob, and licked every bit of him that he
could.

"Here—be careful of Uncle Bob—he's rather
frail at the moment," said Nicky, grinning. "Isn't
he pleased to see you, Uncle! You've come on a
good day—it's the first day of the Easter hols!"

"Good for you!" said Uncle Bob, clapping
Nicky on the back. "You'll be able to take me
for some walks—and maybe we can do some bird-
sleuthing together—you're still keen on birds, I
suppose?"

"Oh *yes*," said Nicky, pleased. "Ken and I
mean to go out bird-watching as usual. We've
heard there's a sparrow hawk somewhere on the
hills, and we'd like to find his nest. Not to take
the eggs," he added hastily, knowing his Uncle's
strict ideas about egg-collecting. "Ken's got an
old pair of field-glasses. Wish *I* had!"

"Well—I might lend you *my* pair," said his
uncle, who was by this time up in his room,
opening his bag. "I always have a pair with me—
useful in my work, you know—and as I shan't be
needing them this time, I'll lend them to you.
That's if you'll promise to care for them as if
they were made of gold! They're jolly fine ones."

"Oh, Uncle Bob! Thanks most awfully!" said
Nicky, overjoyed. "It's not much fun sharing a

pair, you know. Ken always wants to use them when *I'm* longing to—but it's jolly decent of him to lend them to me, anyhow. Now we'll each have a pair. I *say*—are these the ones you use? What *magnificent* field-glasses! I bet Mother'll say you're not to lend them to me!"

Everyone liked Uncle Bob, and as for Mrs. Hawes, she was, as Nicky said, "quite potty on him."

"We always get smashing cakes when *you* come, Uncle," said Nicky, at tea-time, when a grand new fruit-cake appeared on the table. "And I bet we'll get heaps of rissoles now, because Uncle Bob likes them. Shan't we, Mother?"

"Bob always was spoilt," said his mother.

"I wish *I* was," said Nicky. "How did you manage to get spoilt, Uncle Bob?"

"Let's change the conversation," said his Uncle. "Actually, when we were kids, *I* always thought your mother was the spoilt one. Well—what sort of a report did you get for last term, youngster?"

"It hasn't come yet," said Nicky. "Two of the teachers were ill at end of term, so the reports are held up. Horrible! It means I have to shiver in my shoes longer than I need. Don't let's talk about reports! Let's talk about Punch. We're going to teach him a lot of new tricks, Uncle. Will you help?"

" You bet ! " said Uncle Bob, helping himself to a second piece of the fruit-cake. " My word, Lucy, if Mrs. Hawes goes on cooking and baking like this, I shall get so fat I'll have to buy new clothes ! "

Punch was sitting as close to Uncle Bob as he could. He liked his smell. He liked his voice. He liked the firm way in which Uncle Bob patted his head. How wonderful to have his two best friends together—Uncle Bob *and* Nicky !

" I thought I'd teach Punch to fetch people's slippers for them, Uncle," said Nicky. " Think how pleased Dad would be to find his slippers by his armchair each night ! And I could teach him to fetch you your outdoor shoes, Granny ! Then you wouldn't have to go and look for them."

" Hm ! " said Granny. " If Punch is going to be as clever as that, he *will* be a busybody ! I think it would be better to teach him to wipe his feet on the mat when he comes in from a walk—that really *would* be something ! "

" Wuff ! " said Punch, sitting up straight, proud that he was being talked about. He gave Nicky's hand a lick, and then Uncle Bob's. He did so like this family of his ! He gave a happy sigh, and laid his head down on Uncle Bob's foot.

" He's getting a bit soppy," said Nicky, amused. " Biscuit, Punch ? "

Punch stopped being " soppy " at once, and sat

up, barking. "Beg, then; beg properly!" ordered Nicky, and waited for Punch to sit up on his hind legs, front paws waving in the air.

"Not very steady, are you?" said Nicky, and gave him a biscuit.

It really was good to have Uncle Bob in the house. He was always ready for a joke, always ready to give a hand with anything, and full of funny stories about his work, though, of course, he never gave any secrets away. He took Punch for long walks, he went shopping for Nicky's mother, and was quite one of the family.

But there were times when he sat silent by the window, drawing on his pipe, hardly answering anyone who spoke to him. He puzzled Nicky and Ken one rainy morning. They were full of high spirits, and wanted him to join in the fun—but he seemed somehow far away, and didn't even notice when Punch tried to leap on to his knee.

Nicky went to his Mother. " Mother—is Uncle Bob all right to-day ? He's hardly spoken a word."

" Well, I told you he's been overworking," said his mother. " He's been forbidden to do any of his work for some time—and the days must sometimes seem empty to him now that he has no puzzling cases or problems to work out. With a brain like his, he must often be bored to death, not being able to use it. I only wish something interesting would happen, so that he could have something to think about."

" What sort of thing do you mean ? " asked Nicky. " Burglaries—or kidnappings—something like that ? I bet our policeman would be proud to have Uncle Bob's help if anything happened here. But nothing ever does—unless you count things like Mrs. Lane's washing being stolen off her line —or somebody breaking the grocer's window ! "

" No, of course I don't mean things like that,"

said his mother. " I don't really know what I *do* mean—except that Bob needs something to take his mind off himself. It's not like him to sit and mope at times. I think the doctor's wrong. Bob doesn't need time on his hands like this—he wants something to *do*—something to set those brains of his working again, instead of rusting."

This was a long speech for his mother to make. Nicky stared at her, worried. " Would he like to go bird-watching with us ? " he said, hopefully. " Or shall I ask him to help me to teach tricks to Punch ? He'd do anything for Uncle Bob."

" Well—you ask him. See what *you* can do," said his mother. " He can't bear me or Granny to fuss round him—and *I* can't bear to see him sitting there not taking any notice of anything, as he's doing to-day ! Maybe you and Ken can help him more than anyone else can."

Nicky went off with Punch, looking thoughtful. Poor Uncle Bob ! He certainly must miss the exciting life he usually had—tracking down criminals—perhaps hunting a murderer—finding stolen goods ! But what *could* he and Ken do to help ?

" Come on, Punch—we'll find Ken, and see if he's got any good ideas," said Nicky. Off they went to Ken's shed, little knowing what good ideas Ken would have—and what extraordinary things would come of them !

CHAPTER 5

KEN HAS AN IDEA

KEN WAS down in his guinea-pig shed as usual. Penelope was there too, cleaning some garden tools. " Hallo, Ken ! " said Nicky. " Hallo, Penny ! "

Penny didn't answer. " She wants to be called Penelope now," explained Ken. " She won't answer to Penny."

" Oh," said Nicky, astonished. " But, why ? Penelope is rather a silly sort of name—Penny's much nicer."

" Well, if that's what you think, I'll go," said Penny, huffily, and promptly threw down the hoe she was cleaning, and went.

" Good ! " said Ken, with a sigh of relief. " She's been reading an old Greek story about some wonderful person called Penelope, and she rather fancies herself now. Any news ? "

" Yes. A bit," said Nicky. " I want your help, Ken. Stop messing about with those guinea-pigs."

Ken looked solemn at once, and shut the door of the cage. " What on earth's up ? " he said. " You look as solemn as Penny ! "

Nicky began to explain about his uncle. " Mother thinks he's moping now," he said. " You know—misses his work. Hasn't anything to sharpen his brains on. She said that perhaps you and I could think of something interesting to brighten him up."

" He might like my guinea-pigs," said Ken at once. " They're *really* interesting. This one, now, he washes his whiskers just as if . . ."

" Don't be an ass, Ken. Who wants to sit and watch guinea-pigs washing their whiskers ? I'd go potty if I'd nothing better to do than that ! No —I mean something really *exciting*—something to take the place of all the interesting and thrilling puzzles and problems that Uncle Bob has to solve for people, when he's in London."

" Well, let's make up a few for him," said Ken, half-joking. " Let's see now—the ' Mystery of the Lights in the Empty House ! ' or ' Who is the Prisoner in the Cave ? ' or ' What made those strange Noises in the Night ? ' It would be a bit of fun for all of us ! We'd lead him properly up the garden path ! "

" You really are rather a fat-head, Ken," said Nicky. " You *know* we couldn't do things like that." He drummed his heels against the side of the box on which he was sitting. Then he suddenly stopped, and sat up straight. He gave Ken a delighted punch, and stared at him with bright eyes.

Penelope was there too . . . .

" *Now* what's up ? " said Ken, quite surprised.

" Well—it's just that I think you've got hold of a good idea," said Nicky. " It sounded too silly for words when you said all that—but, you know, there *is* something in it ! "

" Wuff ! " said Punch, feeling Nicky's sudden excitement, putting his paw up on the boy's knee.

" You don't mean we *could* make up a mystery for your uncle to solve, do you ? " said Ken, disbelievingly. " He'd be wild when he found out ! Anyway, he'd never believe in it. He'd smell a rat at once."

" Wuff ! " said Punch again, hearing the word " rat ".

" Don't interrupt, Punch," said Nicky, feeling more and more excited. " Ken, it would be *fun* ! We'll work out something between us. Let me see—how could it be done ? I'll have to think."

" Look—we can't deceive your uncle like that," said Ken, really alarmed now. " He'd be furious. Anyway, he's so jolly clever he'd see through it at once. We can't pit our brains against *his* ! "

" We can try ! " said Nicky, red with excitement. " Look—something like this, Ken. We'll get him to come out bird-watching with us— taking our field-glasses, of course. And we'll put clues here and there, see, for him to find."

" You're barmy," said Ken, disgusted.

" I'm not. We could let a piece of paper blow in the wind, and when he picks it up, it's a message in code ! Ha—very mysterious ! And we could get him to train his field-glasses on something peculiar, and . . ."

" Peculiar ? What do you mean, *peculiar* ? " asked Ken, puzzled.

" Oh—someone signalling out of a window or out of that old tower up on the hills ! " said Nicky. " I'm sure Uncle Bob would think that peculiar, and he'd want to find out what was going on."

" Yes. But actually there wouldn't *be* anything going on," said Ken. " And he'd soon find that out."

" Oh shut up finding fault with everything I say," said Nicky, drumming his heels angrily against the box, and making Punch bark again. " I thought you'd be glad to help. Mother said we might think of something together—and here you've come up with a perfectly splendid idea, that would be fun for all of us—and now you pooh-pooh it ! I only wish *I'd* thought of it ! "

Ken began to think he must have been very clever after all. He stopped making difficulties. " Oh well—if you *really* think I've had a brainwave, I'll help. But it's all got to be worked out carefully, mind—this pretend mystery, whatever it

is. And what will your uncle say when he finds
it's all a hoax ? "

" He'll laugh like anything," said Nicky. " He's
got a terrific sense of humour, and he never minds
a joke against himself. We'll be giving him a bit
of excitement, something to puzzle him and take
him out of himself, as Mother says. And what's
more, *we* shall enjoy it too ! Shan't we, Punch,
old thing ? "

Punch hadn't the faintest idea what the boys
were talking about, but he heartily agreed with
everything. He ran round the shed, barking loudly,
and nosed excitedly into every corner.

" He's looking for a deep, dark secret, a hidden
mystery that only Uncle Bob can solve," said
Nicky, in a hollow, dramatic voice that made Ken
laugh, and Punch look up in surprise.

" All right," said Ken. " You think up the
clues. I thought of the idea, so I've done my bit.
Is all this to happen in the daytime or night-time ?
I'm quite game to wander about at night, if you
want me to. Only it's no good asking Mum if I
can—she'd say ' no '."

" For goodness' sake ! You mustn't say *anything*
about this to your mother ! " said Nicky, in horror.
" She'd go and tell *my* mother at once, and that
would be the end of it. We're doing this to help
my Uncle Bob, remember, and NOBODY except

you and me must know about it. And Punch, of course."

" When will you think out the clues we're to spread around? " asked Ken. " I'm beginning to feel excited."

" I think I'd better think about them in bed to-night," said Nicky, sliding off the box. " That's when I get my best ideas. What a laugh we'll have! By the way—I'm teaching Punch some tricks. Like to come and help? I'm teaching him to fetch people's slippers for them. He's already got the hang of it."

" *Really?* Isn't he a marvellous dog? " said Ken, twiddling one of Punch's alert ears. " Yes, I'll come. And listen, Nicky—don't say a word of our plan in front of Penny—Penelope, I mean— you know how snoopy she is."

" As if I would! " said Nicky, scornfully. " Come on, Punch. Come and show what a clever dog you are! "

And, for the next half-hour, Nicky's house echoed to sounds of " Fetch it, then, boy! Grandma's shoes! Up the stairs, Punch! That's right. He's gone to get one, Ken! Buck up, Punch! GRANDMA'S SHOES! "

Down the stairs came Punch at top speed, carrying one of Uncle Bob's bedroom slippers in his mouth. He put it down at Nicky's feet with a look of pride, his tail wagging nineteen to the dozen.

"Ass!" said Nicky. "I said 'GRANDMA'S' not Uncle Bob's. Try again." And up the stairs went Punch, tail down now. He appeared in a few seconds with one of Nicky's football boots, tripping over the laces as he came.

"He's not really very clever, is he?" said Ken. Nicky was puzzled. "I don't understand him. He fetched Grandma's shoes after breakfast all right."

A voice came down the stairs—Grandma's. "Nicky! Please STOP Punch scratching at my door. He can't have my shoes—I'm wearing them!"

"There!" said Nicky, relieved. "I *knew* there was a good reason why he didn't bring them. Good dog, Punch. You shall help us with our secret plan! You're as clever as a bagful of monkeys!"

CHAPTER 6

NICKY MAKES SOME PLANS

FOR ONCE in a way Nicky went off to bed without voicing his usual strong objections. He really was longing to think up some wonderful mystery for his Uncle Bob! His Granny was surprised when he kissed her so early in the evening.

" My, Nicky—you're going early to-night ! " she said. " Are you feeling all right ? "

" Yes. I'm fine," said Nicky. " I just want to

think out something in bed, that's all. 'Night, Mother, 'night, Dad. Come on, Punch."

Punch leapt up, gave everyone a good-night lick, and disappeared out of the door with Nicky.

" Well ! *They're* early to roost to-night ! " said Grandma. " Nicky must be tired."

He wasn't ! He was very wide awake indeed, and his mind was already busily thinking out plans, as he undressed. Punch was surprised that Nicky said nothing to him, for usually he was very talkative. He whined, wondering if he was in disgrace for something, but still Nicky took no notice !

Punch wondered what to do. Why didn't Nicky talk to him as he usually did ? Was he in disgrace ? The little terrier suddenly barked and ran out of the room, his tail wagging. *He* knew how to please Nicky and make him talk to him, he was sure he did ! He came back with a shoe of Uncle Bob's. Nicky didn't even notice ! Punch ran out again, and came back with Mrs. Fraser's bedroom slippers, and set them down beside the shoe. Then off he went again for more !

But Nicky was still lost in thought. He had cleaned his teeth, washed, done his hair—and then by mistake he cleaned his teeth again without even noticing ! That really did surprise Punch !

Nicky leapt into bed, and was just about to put

out his bedside lamp when he caught sight of the seven or eight slippers and shoes that Punch had been fetching to try to please him. There they were, all set out on the bedside rug, Punch lying forlornly with his head on two of them.

" Oh *poor* old Punch ! " said Nicky. " I've not said a word to you for ages ! I've been thinking hard, Punch, and all the time you've been rushing about fetching shoes to please me. *Dear* Punch ! Did you think I was cross with you, or something ? Well, I'm not. I think you're the best dog in the world ! "

Punch went quite mad with joy. He tore round and round the room, sending the shoes flying, barking madly—and then with one final enormous leap he landed on top of Nicky, and licked every inch of his face.

" Oooh, Punch—that was my tummy you jumped on ! " groaned Nicky. " Lie down, you ass. No, you can't get into bed beside me. You know Mother would find you when she came up, and you'd get a smack. Gosh, look at all those slippers and shoes—honestly, you're a mutt. Now just you take them back ! "

But that was a trick that Punch had not yet learnt, and he lay still, licking Nicky's hand every now and again, glad to find that his beloved master was not angry with him after all.

"Now just keep absolutely *quiet*," said Nicky. "I'm going to have one of my THINKS, and I'll push you off the bed if you so much as wriggle your tail."

Punch lay so still that Nicky forgot all about him, and was soon lost in thought. Now then—a smashing mystery was what he wanted—complete with clues, strange goings-on, and all the rest of it—a mystery in which he could make Uncle Bob so interested that he would forget all about being bored and miserable.

Where should the mystery *be*? That was the first thing to think out. At once a picture of an old burnt-out building up on Skylark Hill came into Nicky's mind. Yes—that would be a fine eerie sort of place for a mystery. He thought about it, remembering the blackened, half-fallen walls—the one old tower still standing—the curious spiral stairway of stone that led down into the old cellars, which he and Ken had so often longed to explore.

"My word, yes—*that's* the place for a pretend mystery," thought Nicky, beginning to feel excitement welling up inside him. "Now, what next?—yes, clues. They'd better be in code—an easy code, so that Uncle Bob can decipher it and read the message. And there shall be lights flashing from the tower at night—I'll make Ken go up

there with his torch and flash it—and what about
noises ? If I can get Uncle up to the burnt house,
Ken can hide and make awful groans. Gosh, this
is going to be super. If only I could tell Ken this
very minute ! "

He debated whether to put on his clothes again
and slip over to Ken's. No—he'd probably be in
bed, and if he was asleep nothing in the world
would wake him, not even stones rattling against
his window !

Nicky became so excited as he thought of the
wonderful Mystery that was lying in wait for
Uncle Bob, that he couldn't keep still. He turned
over and over in bed, and Punch was soon tired of
continually being bumped, and leapt down to the
rug, landing on the slippers and shoes.

" We'll begin the Mystery to-morrow," thought
Nicky, sticking his hot feet out of bed to cool
them. " Ow—stop it, Punch—those are my toes
you're biting ! Sh—here comes Mother. Get
under the bed."

Punch disappeared at once. Mrs. Fraser opened
the bedroom door, and the landing light shone
into the room, showing her Punch's surprising
collection of shoes. " So *that's* where my slippers
went to ! " she thought, and picked them up.
" Good gracious—this is quite a shoe-shop ! I'll
have to stop this new trick of Punch's, I can see ! "

She laid her hand gently on Nicky's forehead, for she still felt puzzled about his going off to bed so early. But it was quite cool—Nicky was obviously all right! Picking up a few more shoes she crept out of the room.

Punch came out from under the bed, and climbed carefully up beside Nicky. He gave his face the tiniest lick, heaved an enormous sigh of love, and settled down to sleep.

Nicky gave Punch a pat, and then slid off into his Mystery once more. But now he was getting sleepy, and his thoughts became muddled. He was at the old burnt house—he was climbing up to the tower—a light was flashing there—good gracious, *two* lights—but no, they weren't lights after all—they were the brilliant green eyes of Ken's cat—and now the cat grew simply enormous, and Nicky fled down to the cellar, where immediately some frightful, blood-curdling noises began that made poor Nicky's hair stand on end !

He was so scared that he tried to scream—and immediately found himself sitting up in bed clutching at a growling, most surprised Punch.

" Oh, it was a *dream*, thank goodness ! " said Nicky, thankfully. " I suppose those awful noises I heard in my dream were you snoring or something, Punch Gosh, I was scared ! If our Mystery's going to be anything like as thrilling as my dream about it, we're going to have some fun! Get off my feet, Punch. No wonder I found it difficult to climb up to the tower in my dream—you must have been lying on my feet all the time!"

Punch obligingly slid off Nicky's feet, and lay at the bottom of the bed. His ears twitched as an owl hooted somewhere in the trees at the bottom of the garden. They twitched again, and a small growl came from him when he heard a cat miaowing below the window. Nicky turned over and buried his head in the pillow. He felt wide awake again, and longed for to-morrow to come so that he might tell Ken all his plans.

"Ha, Uncle Bob—you don't know what thrills I've got in store for you!" he murmured. "I'll write out that code message first thing to-morrow and show it to Ken—I bet *he* won't be able to decipher it! And we'll go up to that old burnt-out house and snoop round. I wonder what will come of my Plan for a Mystery—I DO hope it will be a success!"

Success, Nicky? Well, you're certainly going to be *surprised*! It's a wonderful plan of yours—but it may not work out in quite the way you think. So watch out, Nicky, watch out, Ken!

CHAPTER 7

A MYSTERIOUS MESSAGE

As soon as Nicky woke up the next morning he
remembered his wonderful plan of the night before.
He sat up in bed, excited, and Punch began to pull
off the blankets and sheet, trying to make his
master get up and dress.

"All right, all right, Punch—I'm in just as
much a hurry as you are!" said Nicky. "If Ken's
up I could go and tell him my plans before breakfast.
No—*don't* drag the pillow on to the floor. Bring
me my shoes—SHOES, idiot, not boots."

Nicky was soon dressed, and leapt down the
stairs with Punch just in front. They almost
bowled over Mrs. Hawes, who was sweeping the
hall.

"Are you two catching a train or something?"
she demanded. "Stop it, Punch—leave my broom
alone! Nicky, he's got my duster now—if he goes
off with it, I'll . . ."

"Bad dog," said Nicky, sternly. "Drop it, sir!
There—see how obedient he is, Mrs. Hawes.
What's for breakfast? I've got time to go and see
Ken, haven't I?"

" It's kippers for breakfast, and you've about ten minutes," said Mrs. Hawes. " Bless that dog —he's gone off with my floor-cloth now ! "

Nicky grinned and shot off at top speed after Punch. He ordered him to take back the floor-cloth.

" And then come down to Ken's shed," he said. " But DON'T bring any shoes with you. I'm sorry I taught you that trick now."

He squeezed through the hedge and went across to Ken's shed. He could hear him chanting his favourite tune—good—he was there then. He whistled piercingly and Ken at once appeared at the shed door, holding one of his smallest guinea-pigs.

" Hallo ! *You're* early ! " he said. " Anything up ? Get down, Punch, you are *not* going to have guinea-pigs for breakfast."

" Ken ! I've thought out a smashing mystery ! " said Nicky. " Where's Penny ? Not in hearing distance, I hope ? "

" No. She's with Winnie—our cousin, you know. She's come to stay again."

" Not that Winnie who wants to tag on to *us* all the time ? " said Nicky, in dismay.

" The very same," said Ken, gloomily. " She arrived last night, fat as ever. We'll have to look out, or we'll have the girls spying on us all the time—especially Winnie. But I say—why are you up so early ? "

" Because I wanted to tell you about the Mystery I've thought out—the one we're going to pretend is a real one, so that Uncle Bob can have something exciting to think about," said Nicky. " Honestly, Ken, it's really *good*—I tell you, we're going to have some fun. Shut the door, and listen. Punch, sit by the door and bark like mad if you hear footsteps or whispering."

Punch at once sat down by the door, and cocked his ears. " Now we're safe," said Nicky. " Listen, Ken."

And he told his surprised friend all that he had thought of during the night. Ken listened, gaping, taking in all the details, but when Nicky came to the bit where he, Ken, was to go to the old burnt-out house at night and flash a torch, he shook his head firmly.

" No. If anyone's to do that, *you* can. I'd be scared to do that on my own."

" Oh don't make things difficult," said Nicky. " Anyway, we can decide all the details later on. I just HAD to let you know what I'd planned. The first thing to do is to write out a secret message —in code, of course. Then we'll take Uncle Bob for a walk up the hills—and let him find the paper with the message on—and—oh BLOW, there's the breakfast gong. You be thinking out a good secret message. I'll be back after breakfast."

He tore off with Punch barking at his heels, and just managed to be sitting down at the breakfast table before his father arrived.

" You seem out of breath," said his mother, surprised. " Have you been for a walk ? "

" No. Just to see Ken about something important," said Nicky. " Do you want me to do anything this morning, Mother ? I thought I'd ask Uncle Bob if he'd like to go for a walk up on Skylark Hill with me and Ken. We want to go bird-spotting, and Uncle Bob said he'd lend me his field-glasses."

" I'm sure he'd *love* to go with you," said his mother, pleased. " It's such a beautiful morning, it will do him good—and he's always been so fond of birds."

Uncle Bob arrived down a few minutes later, looking rather gloomy.

" Hallo, everyone ! " he said. " No, no kipper for me, thanks. I don't feel too good. Couldn't get a wink of sleep because of the owls hooting all night."

" *I* never heard them," said his sister. " Poor old Bob—you do look washed-out."

" Uncle—come for a walk up Skylark Hill this morning ! " said Nicky, eagerly. " Ken's going too—bird-spotting. We might see the sparrow hawk. You said you'd lend me your field-glasses, remember ? "

" Right. I'll come with you," said Uncle Bob. " Do me good to stretch my legs. What time do you want to start ? "

" Er—would ten o'clock do ? " asked Nicky, remembering that he must leave himself enough time to work out a message in code, so that he could plant it somewhere for his uncle to find.

" That'll suit me fine," said Uncle Bob. " I'll unpack my field-glasses after breakfast—they're still in one of my cases. Is Punch coming with us ? I hope he won't race about and scare all the birds for miles."

" Of course he's coming," said Nicky, feeling a sudden little paw on his knee. He bent down to Punch, who was as usual under the table. " You heard what Uncle Bob said, didn't you, Punch ? No racing about and barking—but plenty of sit, sit, sit, when you're told. Got that ? "

" Wuff," said Punch, quite understanding, and lay down again.

Nicky hurriedly finished his breakfast, trying to think out what message he should write on a piece of paper.

" Please excuse me, Mother," he said. " I've a few things to do before we go."

"Well, remember that one of them is to make your bed, please," said his mother, as Nicky raced off with Punch just behind him.

He went to his bedroom and hurriedly pulled together his sheets and blankets. Then he tore a piece of paper from an old writing pad, sat down and chewed the end of his pencil. What should the message be? Perhaps he had better go and see if Ken had thought of one.

Soon he was down in Ken's shed. "Ken—I *can't* think of a message!" he said. "And Uncle Bob will be ready to go with us at ten. What shall . . .?"

"Don't worry. *I've* thought of one," said Ken, proudly, and showed Nicky a piece of dirty, torn paper. On it he had written a most mysterious-looking message, which looked like this:—

UFMM KJN XFSF SFBEZ. NFFU JO DFM-MBST. TUVGG IJEEFO PO TLZMBSL IJMM. MPPL PVU GPS TJHOBM GSPN UPXFS.

IBSSZ.

"What on earth does *that* mean?" said Nicky.

"It means '*Tell Jim we're ready. Meet in cellars. Stuff hidden on Skylark Hill. Look out for signal from tower. Harry.*'" said Ken, proudly. "It's in an awfully simple code—all I've done is to use the next letter to the real one each time—B for A, C for B, D for C and so on. This first word UFMM, for instance. All you've got to do is to think of the letter before . . ."

"Oh, *I* see—for the letter U the one before would be T—and for F it would be E, and for MM

it would be LL," said Nicky. "The word 'tell' —and so on. Isn't it too simple?"

"No. Don't you think it's an *exciting* message?" said Ken. "I mean—when your uncle picks up this old dirty-looking bit of paper with such a strange code message on it, he's bound to prick up his ears! I rubbed it on the floor of the shed to make it look dirty."

Nicky began to feel excited. "Yes! It's fine!" he said. "I don't know how you thought of such an exciting message. Jolly good, Ken. Look now —when Uncle Bob is training his field-glasses on some bird or other, you drop the bit of paper nearby, and maybe he'll see it and pick it up. If he doesn't I'll pick it up, and pretend to be very puzzled, because of the code. I bet Uncle will decipher it at once."

"And then the fun will begin!" said Ken, his eyes shining. "We'll go exploring the cellars— we'll hunt on the hill for the stuff that's supposed to be hidden there. We'll . . ."

"We'd jolly well better buck up!" said Nicky. "It's almost ten, and I'm not ready yet. Meet me at your front gate as soon as you can. This is going to be fun! I *bet* Uncle Bob will prick up his ears and forget to be mopey, once he gets going on our mystery!"

CHAPTER 8

UP ON SKYLARK HILL

NICKY and Punch raced off to see if Uncle Bob was ready to go for his walk up Skylark Hill. Yes—there he was, waiting impatiently in the front garden, his field-glasses slung over his shoulder.

" Oh, there you are," he said. " Where's Ken ? "

" Just coming—he'll be at his front gate," said Nicky. " Shall I go in and get my bird-book, Uncle ? "

" No. I can tell you anything you want to know," said his uncle. " For goodness' sake let's start while it's fine ! Come along."

They picked up Ken at his front gate and set out happily, Ken with his glasses slung round his shoulder just like Uncle Bob. They came to Skylark Hill, and at first took an ordinary path, Punch running ahead as usual, sniffing about for rabbits.

The birds were singing madly. " There's the chaffinch, with his ' chip-chip-cherry-erry-erry-chippy-oo-EEE-ar ' song," said Uncle Bob, standing to listen. " And you can hear that greenfinch—and the hedge-sparrow—and what's that now, singing so VERY loudly ? "

59

" The wren—look, it's over there ! " said Ken, pointing. " Seems funny that such a *little* bird should have such a very loud voice ! "

It was lovely up on the hill. It was quite a wild part where they were now wandering, no paths at all, except for those made by the rabbits. Uncle Bob suddenly stopped.

" Listen—there's a nightingale singing in that bush over there—see, at the top of that hawthorn bush."

" I thought nightingales only sang at night," said Nicky, astonished.

" Oh no—you can hear them in the daytime too," said Uncle Bob, " though no one notices them much then, with so many other birds singing. We really ought to come up here at night-time to hear them at their best."

Nicky at once gave Ken a violent nudge. What a wonderful excuse for coming out at night ! Perhaps he could make Ken go up unseen to the old tower and flash his torch, while he and Uncle Bob were listening to nightingales ! Uncle Bob would never guess that the flashing light was a put-up job—he would be sure to think there was something funny going on in that old burnt-out place ! He'd smell a mystery at once !

They went on a little way, and soon Nicky thought it was about time that Ken dropped his dirty bit of paper with the code message on it. He nudged him again, and Ken put his hand in his pocket, and nodded.

He went on some way in front, and suddenly spotted a chaffinch's nest in a bush. Ah—now he could perhaps make Nicky's uncle find the paper for himself! That would be very much better than either he or Nicky pretending to find it. He cautiously parted the twigs, and dropped the note into the bushy part below the nest. Then he called to Nicky.

" I say—here's a nest, just newly-built. No eggs yet, though. Ask your uncle what kind of nest it is—looks like a chaffinch's to me."

" Don't disturb the bird if it's on the nest," called Uncle Bob, as he and Nicky came up the steep little rabbit-path. He peered into the bush. " Yes—that's a chaffinch's nest—see how neat it is. The bird has even woven tiny bits of torn paper into it. I wonder it didn't take *this* old bit of paper too, below the nest."

And, much to the boys' delight, he picked up the note that Ken had just dropped into the bush! He saw that something was written on it and glanced idly at it, as he was about to screw it up.

" Hallo—what's this? It's a note written in code! " he said, in surprise.

"I *say!*" said both boys at once, pretending to be astonished. "Code! What's it say?"

"Don't know, unless I can break the code," said Uncle Bob. "It looks a fairly simple one. See what *you* can make of it. I don't feel too bright this morning."

The boys didn't know whether to decipher it or not. Wouldn't Uncle Bob think they were a bit too clever if they did? They sat down and put their heads together, pretending to puzzle over the queer message.

"Look at that first word," said Uncle Bob. "'UFMM'! A double-letter at the end. Now what letters can be doubled at the end of words? S can, for instance. There are plenty of four-letter words ending in double S—fuss, boss, toss, hiss and so on—or in double F—such as huff, muff, etc."

"Or double L," said Nicky. "Such as ball, call, toll, er . . ."

"Or TELL!" said Ken, as if he had just that very minute thought of it. "It might be 'tell,' mightn't it?"

"I should think it's more likely to be 'TELL' than anything else," said Uncle Bob, taking back the paper. "Now, let's see what the next word would be, if the first is TELL—it will mean that the letters of each code word must be replaced by the *preceding* letters of the alphabet. All right— the next code-word is KJN. We'll replace those three letters by the alphabet letters immediately before—that is, K would be J, J would be I, and N would be M—making the word J-I-M—JIM!"

"Aha!" said Ken, "that would make the first two words 'TELL JIM'! You've broken the code already! We shall be able to decipher the whole message now!"

He looked so excited that Nicky stared at him in surprise. Goodness—how clever Ken was at acting! No one would ever think that it was he himself who had actually made up the message and put it into code!

Uncle Bob looked rather startled. He stared at the message again, and stood frowning over it.

" Queer! " he said at last. " That's the code all right—a very simple one, too—listen—I'll decode the whole message."

The boys felt a great desire to giggle. This was marvellous! Dear old Uncle Bob was well and truly taken in! They listened as he slowly read the decoded message.

" Tell - Jim - we're - ready. Meet - in - cellars. Stuff - hidden - on - Skylark - Hill. Look - out - for - signal - from - tower. Harry."

He frowned down at the paper again. " Why did the writer of this message, whoever he is, use such an easily deciphered code? " he wondered. " He might just as well have written it in plain English! I wonder if it *could* be a joke— but if so, how did it come to be in that bush? "

" Perhaps the wind blew it there," suggested Nicky. " Oh Uncle Bob—it's awfully exciting, isn't it? "

Uncle Bob put the paper into his pocket. " Something funny about it," he said. " Funny and phoney! I'll have to think about it."

" Should we try and find whatever stuff it is

that's supposed to be hidden on the hill?" said Ken, feeling nervous in case Uncle Bob should decide it *was* a hoax. "We might find something interesting. Stolen goods—or—or hidden money, perhaps."

"And what about looking in the cellars of that old burnt-out house?" suggested Nicky. "It says something about cellars in that note, doesn't it, Uncle Bob? It might mean the old cellars up in that place on the top of the hill, And it's got a tower, too—a fine tower to signal from!"

"Yes—anyone on the hillside waiting for a signal could easily see flashes from that tower!" said Ken, backing up Nicky valiantly. "I *say*! We can see that tower from our back gardens, you know—we ought to watch out at night, in case someone *does* signal!"

"Well—I must say it all sounds rather queer— and, as I say, I can't help feeling there's something wrong—something phoney about that note," said Uncle Bob, frowning. "It's too easy a code. I'll think about it. In the meantime, what about a little more bird-spotting?"

"Let's go up to the old burnt house," suggested Nicky. "It's quite interesting, Uncle. The tower is still all right—and the cellars too, though an awful lot of walls have fallen."

"Well—we'll have a quick look round." said

his uncle. "But I'm pretty certain that note doesn't mean a thing—probably some silly schoolboy joke. Still, I can see you're longing to do a little exploring, so come along!"

The two boys fell behind Uncle Bob, as he went up the hill. "Do you think he suspects us!" said Nicky, in a low voice. "You heard what he said about 'schoolboy joke.'"

"Yes—but I don't believe he thinks *we* wrote that message." answered Ken. "Come on—it will be fun to explore that old place again."

"Punch! You can't possibly get down that rabbit-hole," called Nicky. "Come along—we're going up to the old cellars—you'll love sniffing round those! You might even find a *rat*!"

Rat? Ah, that made Punch leave his rabbit-hole at once, and tear after Nicky. He hadn't any interest in birds—and there didn't seem to be any rabbits about—but maybe a nice big rat would turn up in those old cellars. Wuff!

CHAPTER 9

"LOOMY AND GLOOMY, GLOWERING AND TOWERING!"

NICKY led the way up to the top of Skylark Hill, following the overgrown path that had once been used by the people who had lived in the great old building at the summit. They came to a gateway, where broken gates hung all askew on their hinges and the old drive that had led to the house was now a mass of strong-growing weeds.

" What a miserable-looking place ! " said Uncle Bob. " It gives me the creeps."

" Wait till you get a good view of the burnt-out building," said Nicky. " That'll give you nightmares ! "

They went up the thickly-weeded drive and past a great clump of pines. Behind these, sheltered from the prevailing wind, stood the great, blackened hulk that had once been a grand mansion, overlooking the countryside with majestic splendour.

Uncle Bob stopped. From the bottom of the hill the old building had merely looked a poor old ruin, its one remaining tower outlined against the sky—but here, at close quarters, it was rather frightening.

" It sort of *looms* at you ! " said Ken.

" Yes—I know exactly what you mean," said Uncle Bob. " It frowns—and glowers—and, as you so rightly say—looms."

" It's loomy and gloomy and glowering and towering, and sulky and hulky," said Nicky, most unexpectedly.

Uncle Bob and Ken stared at him in amazed surprise. " Why, that's poetry ! " said Ken. " Surely you didn't say that out of your own head ? "

" Well, I did," said Nicky, almost as surprised as the others.

" Whether it came out of your own head or not, it just about describes this brooding, blackened old place," said Uncle Bob. " You might give us warning when you're going to break out into verse again, Nicky. I feel almost as surprised as if Punch had suddenly burst into song ! "

" Wuff ! " said Punch, pleased at hearing himself talked about. He ran on in front of them, his tail wagging. He had been here before, and thought it was a most exciting place.

They all went up the curving drive, and came to the great building itself. It was a sorry sight. The fire that had devoured it had swept it from top to bottom, and had left only one tower untouched, though blackened with smoke.

" Birds build in the tower now," said Ken, as

they went towards the fallen archway that had once framed the great front entrance. " And once I saw a badger coming out of a hole in the wall."

" Who lived here ? " asked Uncle Bob. " It must have been a wonderful place."

" Somebody foreign," said Nicky, trying to remember. " A prince from the East somewhere."

" It had a magnificent view ! " said Uncle Bob. " I wonder what caused the fire."

" Nobody knows," said Ken. " All the people down in the valley awoke one night to see flames reaching up into the sky—and not a single fire-engine could get up this hill to do anything to help. It just burnt to a shell. Everyone in it escaped, and went back to their own country— they were nearly all foreigners. The prince never came back."

" So there it is—just a hulk of a place ! " said Nicky. " Most people are scared of coming up here to it. Like to see the cellars ? "

" Yes—we'd better, as the writer of that peculiar message—what was the name he signed now— Harry—mentioned something about cellars, didn't he ? " said Uncle Bob. He walked into what must once have been a great hall. The floor was still paved with stone, though it was now cracked and blackened, and weeds grew up in the crevices.

Nicky pointed to a burnt mass of wood hanging from one of the walls.

" That was the staircase—or one of them," he said. " But the tower had a stone stairway, so it wasn't burnt. A good many of the stone stairs have got broken, though—perhaps the heat cracked them, or something. Some of them are missing, so you have to be careful in climbing up."

He led his Uncle to a far corner of the old hall, and in at a small stone-arched doorway. " Here's the tower ! " he said. " And that's the stone stair up to it, going round and round the walls—not very safe, is it ? "

" Have you ever been up ? " asked Uncle Bob, going up the first few steps.

" Oh, yes ! " said Nicky. " There used to be an iron rail fixed into the wall—there's still some of it left—so you can hang on to that when you come to the broken-away bits."

Uncle Bob began to ascend the narrow stone stair. He went very gingerly indeed, for much of the stone was breaking away, and he didn't want to plunge downwards. The boys followed.

When they came at last to the top, and were able to look through one of the great square stone windows through which the wind blew cold and strong, Uncle Bob gave a low whistle.

" My word ! WHAT a view ! All round the

hill, and down into the valleys for miles and miles."

"What a place to signal from, too!" said Ken, giving Nicky a nudge. "Flashes from this tower could be seen for a long way, couldn't they?"

"Oh—you're thinking of that code-message," said Uncle Bob. "What was it now—'look out for signal from tower' or something. Yes—certainly this would be a good signalling place. But I don't imagine that anyone would want to come all the way up to this windy tower to do a spot of signalling that hundreds of people could see—if they happened to be looking!"

"I say—look—there's a dead match on the floor here," said Nicky, suddenly, and picked one up. "Would that belong to some signaller, do you think?"

Uncle Bob laughed. "No! To some innocent sightseer like ourselves, ass! Anyone would think you really did believe that message! I tell you, I'm pretty sure it's phoney—just a silly schoolboy joke."

"Where's Punch?" said Ken, hurriedly changing the subject. "Didn't he come up with us?"

"No—he doesn't much like the noise of the wind up here," said Nicky. "Don't you remember how scared he was before, when we brought him up, and the wind whistled all round him! He shot down again so fast that he rolled down the last dozen steps, and then sped off down the hill at sixty miles an hour! Let's go down and find him. He'll be lonely."

So they left the magnificent view and went carefully down the stone stairway, calling to Punch as they came near the bottom. But no answering bark came, no patter of eager feet.

" PUNCH! " yelled Nicky. " Where are you? Surely you haven't gone home without us? "

Not a sound was to be heard, except for the hoarse croaks of crows flying round the tower. Punch was nowhere to be seen!

" Where on earth has the idiot gone? " said Nicky, puzzled. " Can he have gone down the spiral stairway to the cellars? Not without us, surely? "

" Where *is* this spiral stairway? " asked Uncle Bob, looking all round.

" In the kitchen part of the building," said Ken, and led the way through a great doorway, one side of which had fallen in, through a passage, and into what must have been the kitchen.

The boys called loudly as they went. " Punch! PUNCH! Where are you? "

" Here's the cellar-door," said Ken. " At least here is where it *used* to be before it was burnt off its hinges! "

A narrow stone doorway led into an equally narrow passage. Nicky produced a torch, and shone it before him. " Better go carefully, Uncle," he said. " These steps are pretty steep—and slimy, too, because they're rather damp. See how they go round and round in a spiral ? "

It was indeed a curious spiral stairway, and dangerous too. Uncle Bob wished there was a hand-rail to hold on to ! At last, after treading warily down what seemed to be at least fifty curving stone steps, they reached the bottom.

" What a horrible place ! " said Uncle Bob, shivering. It was pitch-black, cold, and rather smelly. " Surely Punch didn't come down here ? "

But he *was* down there ! From what seemed to be a great distance, his bark came echoing up to them, sounding weird and hollow—and scared !

" PUNCH ! Come here ! PUNCH ! " shouted Nicky.

But Punch didn't come. Only his bark came to their ears, a frightened, pleading bark. Whatever was the matter ?

" Come on—I'm going to find him ! " said Nicky, and flashed his torch around, to see which was the best way to go. " Something's happened to old Punch. He sounds quite lost. I simply MUST go to him ! "

CHAPTER 10

A BIT OF EXCITEMENT

" WAIT A MINUTE ! " said Uncle Bob. " Do you know your way about these cellars ? It seems a pretty vast place down here to me, from what I can see by the light of your torch. Passages leading off everywhere ! We might easily get lost."

" Once we find Punch he'll lead us back to the

spiral stairway all right," said Nicky. " Listen—
he's barking again."

They went along a dark, low-roofed passage and
came into yet another cellar, heaped with old
rubbish. The fire had not reached down into the
cellars, so the old boxes and junk had not been
burnt. And then, just at that moment, Nicky's
torch went out ! They were in complete darkness.

" Battery's gone," said Nicky, in disgust. " If
only Punch would come to us, and show us the
way back ! PUNCH ! COME HERE ! "

But no Punch came—and what was almost worse,
he stopped barking ! Not a sound came up the dark
passages, and Nicky felt scared. What could have
happened to make Punch stop barking ?

Uncle Bob took matters in hand at once. He
took Nicky firmly by the arm, and pushed him
back towards the way they had come. " No more
nonsense," he said. " If we go down there any
farther in complete darkness, we shall lose our
way, and not know how to get back."

" But I CAN'T leave Punch by himself," pro-
tested Nicky, trying to wriggle away from his uncle's
firm hand.

" If he went down there, he can come up
again," said Uncle Bob. " Anyway, we are ALL
going back at once ! I'm a bit afraid we shall miss
our way even the short distance we came, it's

so dark. Ken—are you there? Keep close to us."

" I'm just behind, sir," said Ken, who felt only too thankful to be going back.

At last they were up in the kitchen again, having found the spiral stairway very difficult indeed to climb in total darkness. " Whew ! " said Uncle Bob, sitting down hard on the wide window-sill that ran round the great kitchen. " Whew! I don't particularly want to go down *there* again ! "

Nicky was almost in tears over Punch. He spoke sullenly to his uncle.

" I think we're cowards, leaving Punch down there. What are we going to do about it ? "

" We'll wait here for a bit and see if he comes back by himself," said Uncle Bob. " If he doesn't we'll go home and get lanterns or more powerful torches. But I don't think we need worry. Punch will appear soon."

Uncle Bob lighted a cigarette and wandered about a little. The boys sat sulkily on the old stone sill, ears open for Punch, eyes on the entrance to the cellars.

Suddenly Nicky leapt to his feet. " I can hear Punch barking ! Listen ! "

Sure enough a barking was to be heard in the distance. Nicky ran to the cellar-entrance—but the barking wasn't coming from there ! It came nearer and nearer. Ken looked out of the open window-arch, and gave a shout.

" He's coming up the drive. Look, there he is, absolutely filthy! Punch! PUNCH! Here we are ! "

Punch gave a delighted volley of barks, raced into the old building, and hurled himself on Nicky, smothering him with dirt and licks. Nicky hugged him.

" Where have you been, you dirty little dog? We thought you were down in the cellars."

" He *was*," said Uncle Bob. " And as he certainly didn't return up the spiral stairway, as *we* did, how on earth did he get out ? '

" Down a rabbit-hole ? " suggested Ken. " I never heard of any *secret* way out of the cellars. Must have been a rabbit-hole ! You rascal, Punch ! We almost got lost for good down those cellars because of you ! "

Punch was hungry. He barked and tugged at Nicky's sleeve, trying to pull him along. Nicky patted him.

" All right, all right, we're all coming. I'm as hungry as you are ! What about you, Uncle Bob ? "

" Well, yes—I must say that for the first time since I came to stay with you, I feel really hungry ! " said Uncle Bob. " We've certainly had an interesting morning—and what with that rather strange

coded message—and all the birds we saw—and
exploring this gloomy old building—I feel that life
has become quite exciting again ! "

The boys were pleased. They looked closely at
Uncle Bob, and decided that he already looked more
like the cheerful, amusing man he had always seemed
to be.

" Our trick worked, didn't it ? " said Ken, in a
low voice to Nicky, as they went back down Skylark Hill. " But I wish your uncle believed more
in that message of ours—I don't want our plan to
come to a sudden end. It's been fun so far."

" The thing that puzzles *me* is how Punch got
out of those cellars," said Nicky. " I suppose he
did find a rabbit-warren and went through it and
found a hole into the open air. But usually he's
too big for any rabbit-hole."

" Well, what else could he have done ? " said
Ken. " I didn't much like going so far down those
cellars. I couldn't help being glad there wasn't
really any mysterious " Harry " waiting down there
to meet his men."

" Harry ? Harry who ? " said Nicky, and then
remembered the made-up message, and laughed.
" Oh, of course—the Harry who was supposed to
sign that message ! Well, Punch would have given
him a bit of a fright, wouldn't he ? "

Penny and her friend Winnie were standing at

Ken's front gate as he and Nicky and Uncle Bob came up. "Hallo, hallo!" said Uncle Bob. "And what have you two girls been up to this morning? You ought to have come with *us*. My word, we've had an exciting time, what with finding a strange message in code, hidden in a bush—and exploring that great burnt building— and seeing Punch disappear down into the cellars, and . . ."

"Oh PLEASE, Uncle Bob—don't give away our secrets," said Nicky, in a low voice, horrified to think that Penny and Winnie should be told all this. They were both agog at once, of course, and to the boys' despair and disgust Uncle Bob actually took out the coded message and showed it to the two excited girls.

"Oooh!" said Winnie, her eyes big with amazement. "Is it a *real* message? Not just one made up by the boys? Once Ken did a message rather like this, and . . ."

"Shut up!" hissed Ken, and gave poor Winnie such a hard pinch that she screamed and ran straight in through the gate, holding her arm. Uncle Bob stared after her in amazement.

"What's the matter with your friend all of a sudden?" he asked, but Penny, seeing Ken's grim look, decided not to say anything about the pinch. Fortunately the sound of a gong being violently struck by Mrs. Hawes in Nicky's hall, brought such delicious thoughts of dinner that Nicky and his uncle at once walked smartly to the front gate, and up the path, followed by an even more hungry Punch.

"It was *mean* of you to show the girls that secret message," Nicky couldn't help saying to his uncle.

"What on earth's *secret* about it?" said his uncle, astonished. "Anyone might have found it! Anyway it's probably a hoax, so cheer up. There *won't* be any meeting in the cellars—there *won't* be any flashing of signals in the tower. There are *no* goods hidden on the hill."

Nicky frowned and set his teeth. "Oh, won't there!" he thought. "You just wait and see, Uncle Bob! You'll be surprised! And very soon too! I'll just pay you out for showing our secret message to those girls! You just wait!"

It was a pity Uncle Bob couldn't read Nicky's angry thoughts. He didn't even know that the boy felt so angry, or he would have been gentler to him. Poor Nicky! He had only thought of the mystery just because he wanted to *help* his uncle—and now everything had gone wrong—and those GIRLS knew about the message!

He sat rather silent at dinner-time, pondering what to do next. Could he possibly persuade Ken to go and signal from the tower at night—and then he, Nicky, could wake his uncle and tell him to look at the flashes. *That* would make him sit up and take notice! "It's no good *me* going to the tower," thought Nicky. "Because someone has got to tell Uncle about the signalling—and he'd think it funny if Ken came to him in the middle of the night—and I wasn't anywhere to be found. Oh blow! I do hope this plan isn't going wrong. Ken will simply HAVE to go and do the signalling. He can take old Punch with him, if he's afraid. Yes—that's a *good* idea."

"You're very quiet this meal-time, Nicky," said his mother. "What are you thinking about so deeply?"

"He's pondering over a very strange message, I expect!" said Uncle Bob, laughing. "Am I right, Nicky?"

"NO!" said Nicky, so fiercely that everyone jumped, and Punch began to bark. "You wait and see, Uncle—I bet that message was right. You just wait and see!"

CHAPTER 11

QUITE A FEW THINGS HAPPEN!

AFTER DINNER was over Nicky disappeared. "Where's he gone?" said his mother. "He seems rather down in the dumps. What happened this morning, Bob?"

"Oh nothing much," said Uncle Bob. "We did some bird-spotting—and found a strange message in a bush—and explored that old burnt-out place—and almost lost Punch in the cellars. Nicky seemed a bit cross because when we met Penelope, Ken's sister, and her friend, I told them what we'd been doing."

"How silly of Nicky to be cross about that!" said Mrs. Fraser. "But he and Ken can't bear the girls knowing about their doings. Penny is a bit of a snooper, from what I hear."

Nicky was certainly feeling cross. After all their trouble in making up a super-mystery, Uncle Bob had laughed at it, and almost given it away! He made up his mind to go across to Ken's and find out whether the girls had wormed anything out of him. Ken wasn't very clever at keeping things from Penny!

Ken wasn't in the shed—but *somebody* was! Nicky shushed Punch, afraid he would bark, and went to peep in at the window. Penny and her friend Winnie were there, poring over a piece of paper, and giggling.

What could be so amusing about it? Nicky longed to know. Then a horrid thought struck him. Had the two girls found the first rough copy of that coded message? Had they looked in the drawer of the old table in the shed, where Ken kept his things? He ran up to the house to find Ken, and ask him where he had left the copy. If the girls knew all about their mystery, he and Ken might as well give up their little joke on Uncle Bob.

Ken was in his room, reading. He was very pleased to see Nicky and Punch. " Hallo ! Anything up ? You look upset," he said.

Nicky told him what he had just seen. " Those *tiresome* girls ! " said Ken, in a rage. " I thought they were going for a walk, so I didn't bother to hide that first rough copy of the coded message. I felt sure they'd do a bit of snooping sometime—but they *said* they were going for a walk, so I didn't rush down to the shed to hide my things ! "

" Well, we'd better give up the whole idea," said Nicky, very angry. " And I jolly well hope you'll knock their silly heads together when they come in."

" What's Punch doing under my bed ? " said
Ken. " He's chewing my new slippers ! Come on
out, Punch, and behave yourself. Go on down and
chase the girls out of the shed."

Almost as if he understood what Ken had said
Punch ran to the door, pushed it open with his
nose and disappeared. All right—if he couldn't
play with Ken's slippers, he'd go and find someone
else's. *He* wasn't going down to the shed ! He
slipped into the room that the two girls shared
and was faced with a most wonderful array of
shoes of all kinds ! He sniffed at a pair of fur boots,
and settled down to chew them in peace and quiet.

The boys began to play a game of cards, but
after a few minutes the thought of the two girls
messing about in his shed was too much for Ken.
" Let's go and give them a fright and turn them
out," he said. " Come on." So down the stairs
they went, and out into the garden. When they
came to the shed it was empty !

" Blow them ! Where have they gone ? " said
Ken. " And where's the rough copy of that secret
message ? Here it is in my drawer—they'll pretend
they never found it or read it ! "

Punch arrived at that moment, carrying the fur
boot he had been chewing. " Where did you get
that, Punch ? " said Nicky, sternly. Punch ran
out into the garden with it, and Nicky was just

going after him when the two girls came running up to the shed, pretending to be very excited.

"Ken! Nicky! What do you think we've found! A note! A secret message—just like the one you found up on the hills. See what it says—let's decode it, quickly."

"We found it under a bush," said Winnie. "Who *could* have put it there!"

"Idiots!" said Ken, angrily. "You can't spoof *us*!"

"It says we're to watch out for a man with a limp," said Penny. "And it's . . ."

"You made it all up yourselves and hid it, so don't tell such whopping stories," said Ken.

"Was *your* message true then?" asked Winnie, giggling. "Go on—do tell us. We're certain you made *yours* up!"

Penny gave a sudden shriek, and pointed at Punch. "Winnie! He's got one of your best fur boots! He's chewing it! Drop it, Punch, drop it!"

She made a dart at Punch, who picked up the fur boot and danced away with it, out of the shed. This was a lovely game! The two girls chased him up the garden and round the pond. Punch suddenly stopped and very neatly dropped the boot into the water, where it bobbed for a few seconds and then sank.

Winnie angrily picked up a stick and ran after Punch, who at once disappeared through the hedge. " If you bring that dog of yours here again I'll— I'll put him in the dustbin ! " she shouted. " He's *ruined* my new boot ! "

The boys decided to leave the two angry girls to themselves. They went through the hedge, grinning at one another. " Clever old Punch ! The way he dropped Winnie's boot into the water— splash ! Just as if he were saying, ' Sucks to you ! There goes your boot ! ' " said Ken. " I vote we give him a jolly good bone or something."

" There are some sausages in the larder," said Nicky. " I'll get him one if Mrs. Hawes is out of the way."

And a little later, a most surprised Punch was eating a really delicious sausage, and being patted and petted. Well ! If dropping people's shoes into the pond produced sausages to eat, Punch was quite willing to drop any amount into all the ponds in the district !

Winnie and Penny were quite determined not to make up their quarrel with the boys. " We'll just ignore them," said Penny. " Letting Punch drop your boot into the pond like that ! They'll be telling him to drop in our hats next and goodness knows what. He's a most annoying dog ! "

So, much to Ken's relief, the girls ignored him

and said nothing to him at all. They played a game of cards by themselves after tea, watched television until supper, and then went up to their room to read.

But that night something happened to make the girls change their minds about not speaking to Ken. They were both in bed, and had been asleep for some time, when a screech owl suddenly screamed outside. They both woke up with a jump.

" Blow that owl ! It *will* sit in that tree at night below our window and screech its head off ! " said Penny, crossly. She jumped out of bed to frighten it away, and it flew off on silent white wings. Penny glanced idly out into the night. Her room was at the back of the house, and looked across the fields to Skylark Hill. Penny was just about to turn back to bed when something caught her eye. What was that flashing on the top of Skylark Hill ? It must be a light in the old tower !

" It's those boys ! " she thought. " Ken and Nicky must be up there, playing a silly trick. That was one of the things in the silly secret message we found in Ken's drawer—signals from the old tower ! Winnie—are you awake ? There's a light flashing from the tower—those two boys must actually have gone up there to do what that silly message said ! "

" But what on earth *for* ? " said Winnie, astonished. " Anyway, it's surely too late for the boys to be out, Penelope ! It's half-past eleven ! "

" I'll see if Ken's in bed," said Penny and went to the room across the passage, where Ken slept. She pushed open the door and switched on the light. To her amazement Ken was in bed and asleep! Could it be *Nicky* up in the tower, then, all alone ? She shook Ken awake.

" What is it ? What's up ? Penny, what's the matter ? " mumbled Ken, sitting up, rubbing his eyes.

" Ken—there's a light signalling from the old tower on Skylark Hill," said Penny, fearfully. " Just like you said it would in your secret message. Ken, can Nicky be up there, all alone ? If not— who is it ? "

Ken shot out of bed and went into Penny's room. He looked through the window—and had a real shock when he saw the flashes coming from the old tower up on the hill. He stared as if he couldn't believe his eyes !

" It *can't* be Nicky ! " he said, quite dazed. " He would have told me if he'd planned to do anything like that. Penny, there's something queer about this. There is really."

" That's what *I* think," said Penny. " You'll have to tell Uncle Bob in the morning. But I bet he won't believe you. *He* didn't believe that silly message of yours. It *was* a made-up one, wasn't it—all pretence ? "

" Oh shut up ! " said poor Ken. " I'm going to dress and go over to Nicky's. I'll throw some stones at his window and see if I can wake him. If he doesn't come I'll climb up the tree just outside and see if he's in bed. If he's not—well—he must be up in that tower. Whew ! Better him than me ! I'd be scared stiff. Get back to bed, Penny. I'll just drag on a few clothes, and I'll be off to Nicky's."

In a few minutes' time, Ken was letting himself quietly out of the back door, and running down the garden to creep through the hedge. Would he find Nicky in bed—or not ? And if he *were* in bed, what in the world was happening up on Skylark Hill ?

CHAPTER 12

AN ADVENTUROUS NIGHT

KEN WAS soon under Nicky's bedroom window, which was at the front of the house. He scraped about in the gravel path there, and gathered a few small stones. He threw them up one by one, missing the window with all but two, which hit the glass with a sharp click. Nicky was fast asleep, and didn't stir. As a rule not even a thunderstorm would wake him!

But someone else stirred—someone who pricked up his ears at the very first sound! Punch was on Nicky's bed as usual, and he growled when he heard the soft sound of footsteps outside. He growled even more when a stone struck the window! Then he gave a sharp bark, and tugged at the blanket which was tucked in round Nicky's neck.

Nicky awoke. " Shut up, Punch! What do you think you're doing ? " he said, sleepily. Punch tugged at his sleeve as he sat up, rubbing his eyes.

Click! That was another small stone against the window. Punch growled again and ran across the room, standing up with his paws on the sill.

" Is there somebody about ? " said Nicky, waking up properly now. He leapt out of bed and joined Punch at the window. " Anybody there ? " he called.

" Sh ! " said Ken's voice from below. " It's me, Ken. I'm coming up the tree, Nicky. Give me a hand at the top, will you ? I've some startling news ! "

He climbed the tree carefully. It wasn't easy in the dark. Nicky took his torch and shone it down the tree to give him a little light. Ken was most relieved when he was at last on the sill.

" What's up ? " asked Nicky.

" There's someone up at the old tower—flashing lights," said Ken. " Penny's bedroom faces that way, and she saw them and came to wake me. At first she thought it might be us up there on the hill—carrying out what we'd said in that code-message! Who on earth can it be? I did think for a moment it might be you—but you wouldn't go without telling me, of course! "

" Ken! This is *extraordinary*! " said Nicky. " I mean—we go and make up a mystery—and put in signals from the tower—and it comes true! Look—are you *sure* that you saw flashes? I mean —you might have been half-asleep or something."

" Well, I wasn't," said Ken. " Nor were the girls. Look—let's go into a room where we get a view of Skylark Hill and the tower—we can't see them from your window."

" Wuff! " said Punch, annoyed because Ken and Nicky were taking absolutely no notice of him. He was delighted to see Ken in the middle of the night, but neither of the boys had even patted his head! They were too puzzled and excited to fuss over Punch!

" Now you be quiet, Punch, and don't growl or whine or *anything*." ordered Nicky, in a low voice. " Stay here for a minute. We'll be back soon."

He and Ken stole across the passage to an empty

room at the back of the house—but alas, a tree was just in front!

" Blow! " said Nicky.

" Well, let's go into another room," said Ken.

" They're all occupied," said Nicky. " Uncle Bob's got the spare room. We might steal into his if he's asleep. I daren't wake up Dad."

" Come on, then," said Ken. So Nicky led him down a passage to another door. They listened outside. To their delight little snores came from inside—yes, Uncle Bob was well and truly asleep!

They turned the door-handle carefully, and crept in. A lamp in the street outside gave a faint light to the room, which had its curtains pulled right back. The boys avoided some clothes on the floor and tiptoed to the window, glad that the curtains were drawn back. They pressed their noses to the glass, and looked towards Skylark Hill. Faintly outlined against the night-sky was the old tower —and as the two boys watched, they saw a sudden sharp flick of light, then another and another.

" There you are! " said Ken, in excitement. " See that—and that! If that's not someone signalling I'd jolly well like to know *what* it is! "

The light from the street lamp caught some glassy surface in the room, and Nicky realised what it was.

" Look—Uncle's field-glasses are over there in

that corner—let's borrow them and see if we can focus them on the tower and see more clearly what's going on! "

In his haste to get the field-glasses Nicky fell over some shoes on the floor, and knocked against the bed. Uncle Bob awoke at once—the bed creaked as he sat up in alarm.

" Who's there? What is it? "

" It's all right, Uncle Bob—it's only us—me and Ken," said Nicky.

Uncle Bob switched on his bedside light and stared at the boys in the greatest astonishment.

" What in the world are you doing? " he asked. " And what's *Ken* here for, in the middle of the night? Or am I dreaming? "

" Uncle Bob, listen! " said Nicky, keeping his voice low. " Someone's signalling from the tower on Skylark Hill—it looks as if he's signalling with a powerful torch."

" Now look here, my boy—don't let's have any more of this silly nonsense," said Uncle Bob, annoyed. " I'm pretty certain you and Ken made up that coded message—the look on your faces gave you away! I didn't mind playing along with you for a joke—but when it comes to you both invading my bedroom in the middle of the night, talking about someone signalling from the tower, it's just TOO MUCH! "

"Didn't you believe our message then?" said Nicky, feeling very small.

"Look—I'm a private detective in real life, as you very well know!" said Uncle Bob. "And I'm not likely to be taken in by a joke invented by a couple of silly schoolboys. Clear out of my bedroom, and don't let's hear any more of this nonsense."

"But *listen*, Uncle Bob," said Nicky, desperately. "We DID see lights in the tower—so did the two girls. Look, you get your field-glasses and focus them on the tower. I bet you'll get as much of a surprise as we did."

"I simply don't believe a word of it," said Uncle Bob, reaching for his field-glasses. "And I very much resent you two boys invading my bedroom in the middle of the night and telling me fairy tales!"

He got out of bed with the field-glasses, and went to the window. He focused the glasses carefully on the tower. and stared for so long that the boys felt impatient.

"Can you see lights flashing?" asked Nicky, at last.

Uncle Bob lowered the glasses and turned on the two anxious boys.

"NO!" he said. "There's not a thing to be seen. Just as I thought! You both deserve a good hiding for coming into my room like this at night

—you really must think I'm a bit of a fool to play such idiotic tricks on me. Now, clear out, and be your age! "

" But Uncle *Bob*," began Nicky, desperately. " I tell you we did see some . . ."

" Oh shut up and go away," said Uncle Bob, and gave the boys a hard push. Ken wriggled away and went to the window for a quick look at the tower. Alas—Uncle Bob was right—all was darkness there now. Whoever had been signalling had stopped flashing his torch or lantern. What bad luck!

" Come on, Nicky," said Ken, and the two boys went out of the room, dismayed and angry. Whoever would have thought that Uncle Bob would treat them like that?

The boys sat on Nicky's bed, an excited Punch between them, and talked sorrowfully about Uncle Bob's utter disbelief.

" Anyway, there *is* something going on up there," said Ken. " And *we'll* go and find out what it's all about. We made up a mystery—and it seems to be coming true! That's strange—but strange things do happen."

" All right. We'll keep Uncle Bob out of it all," said Nicky. " We'll solve everything ourselves. We'll take Punch up to the tower to-morrow and scout round for all we're worth! We'll show

Uncle Bob we're better detectives than he is! But gosh—I hope he doesn't tell Dad about all this. I'd get into trouble, I bet I would."

" Cheer up—he won't say a word." said Ken, comfortingly. " He's angry with us—but he's not mean enough to get us into trouble! I rather wish we hadn't made up that mystery now! "

" Well, *I'm* not," said Nicky. " If we hadn't thought of it, we'd never be solving this one, would we? You go back home now, Ken—we'll talk about this to-morrow."

" We'll have to tell the girls, you know, Nicky," said Ken. " I mean—it was they who saw the lights flashing from the tower. We can't keep them out of things now."

" Oh blow it! " said Nicky. " I suppose we can't. But they're not to come up to the tower with us, Ken. I won't have that! What we do, we do on our own."

" All right," said Ken, climbing out of the window. " I'll leave *you* to argue with them about that. So long, Nicky! Sleep well! "

And down the tree he went. What a truly adventurous night!

CHAPTER 13

EXCITING PLANS

THE GIRLS were both fast asleep when Ken crept back into his room, so he didn't disturb them—he was, in fact, very thankful not to have to explain what had happened.

He jumped into bed, puzzled about the lights in the tower for a few seconds, and then fell into a deep sleep. Penny woke him up in the morning by shaking him violently, and demanded to know whether it was Nicky who had been up to the tower and was playing about there in the night.

" No, it wasn't," said Ken. " And get out of my room. Can't you wait till I'm dressed? I'll tell you everything then, though I don't really think you deserve to come in on this, after all your snooping."

" Oh Ken—we won't snoop any more," said Penny. " But Ken, was that secret message of yours REAL, not made-up? How did you know about the lights in the tower—I mean, you must have known *something*, to put that in the message, if you did make it up."

" You're muddling me," said Ken. " For goodness' sake stop talking and let me get up. We'll have a meeting down in the shed after breakfast."

And so, at ten o'clock when the girls had done their household jobs, they went down the garden to the shed, to join the boys. Ken was already there, cleaning out the guinea-pig cage, and Nicky was just arriving with Punch.

Nicky took charge at once, determined not to let the girls get out of hand.

" Now just listen, everyone," he said. " You two girls know that Ken and I made up a mystery to interest Uncle Bob, and make him forget about being overworked. *We* wrote out that message, Ken put it into code—jolly clever of him—and we dropped it into a bush on Skylark Hill. That's where Uncle Bob found it—and he *seemed* to believe it, I must say."

"I bet he didn't really," said Winnie, with a giggle. "He wouldn't have shown it to *us*, if he'd *really* believed it."

"Shut up, Winnie," said Ken, sharply, and Winnie subsided, with a grin spreading over her plump face.

"Well," went on Nicky, "you two girls saw lights in the tower last night, and you told Ken, and he came over to me—and we *both* saw them, of course. We had to go in to Uncle Bob's room to see them, and he woke up, and . . ."

"Ooooh! Did *he* see them too?" asked Penny. "Whatever did he say? I bet he believed in your mystery then!"

"Will you PLEASE not interrupt?" said Nicky, exasperated. "He *didn't* see them! The beastly signals had stopped by the time he got to the window—and so he doesn't believe us—he thinks we made up the flashing signals, and he's so angry that he won't listen to a single word about any mystery now, real or otherwise!"

"Gosh!" said Penny. "What are we going to do, then? I mean—your pretend mystery's turned into a *real* one, hasn't it? *Someone* must have been up there in the tower last night—up to no

good—and there are others in the mystery too—
the people he was flashing to. And what was he
signalling about—and why—and . . .?"

" All right, all right, Penny," said Ken. " Just
hold your tongue for a minute—if you *can*—and
let Nicky get on. It's only because you saw the
flashes last night, and were decent enough to tell
me, that we're letting you come in on this."

" And what's more we're going to tell you any
future plans we make," said Nicky. " You'll have
to be in on this now that you know so much—
BUT—you've got to take orders from *me*, and do as
you are told, see ? "

" Right," said Winnie, glowing with excitement. " Oooh, Nicky—you do sound grown-up.
I'll do exactly what you say ! You will, too, won't
you, Penny ? "

" I don't know about *that*," said Penny. " I'll
back up the boys—but I'm going to have *my* say
in the matter, too."

" WUFF ! " said Punch, sitting up straight as
if he thoroughly agreed with all this.

" Now, don't *you* start airing your views, too,"
said Nicky, giving Punch a tap on the head. " It's
bad enough coping with two girls without *you*
entering into the argument as well ! "

That made everyone laugh. Ken went to his
cupboard and took out a packet of toffees.

" All this talk is making me hungry," he said. " Have some, girls? No, not you, Punch, old thing. Have you forgotten what happened to you last time you chewed up some toffees? You lost your bark for ages because your teeth got stuck together!"

Winnie giggled. " Oh I *wish* I'd seen him! Now do let's go on with your plans. What are you going to do about this mystery? What do you *think* is going on?"

" Well—I really haven't the faintest idea," confessed Nicky. " I've just thought of the usual things you know—thieves—or somebody captured and imprisoned up there, perhaps—or someone hiding there for some reason—perhaps an escaped prisoner . . ."

" Ooooh!" said Winnie, her eyes round with excitement. " Go on, Nicky!"

" Whatever it is, we're going to find out," said Ken, firmly. " And though we'll let you girls know what we're doing, you are NOT going to be mixed up in this."

" We'll see about that," said Penny.

Ken put the toffee bag well out of Punch's reach, and sat down. " *I* think the first thing to do is to try and find out who was up there signalling last night—see if he left any traces—try to find where he was hiding—and that means that Nicky and I go up there for the day—take a picnic lunch, and do a bit of spying."

"We ought to go down into the cellars again and look round," said Nicky. "We couldn't look round properly yesterday because my torch battery went phut. There might be some very interesting clues down there!"

"Gracious—I hope you'll be careful!" said Penny. "Do you remember old Harriet, our daily woman? Well, her sister is caretaker at the local museum here, and one day when we were there, she showed us some old plans of that burnt-out place—plans made before it was destroyed, of course—and you should have seen the plans of the cellars—gosh, they seemed to go half down the hill!"

"REALLY!" said Nicky, sitting up at once. "Look, there's something you girls could do—go and have a look at the plans—perhaps copy them very simply—and see what else you can find out. There may be some secret hiding-place, for instance, which might still be there. *Somebody* must be hiding up there, that's certain!"

"Right," said Penny, delighted. "We'll do that this very morning. We'll go now!"

She jumped up, and Winnie got up too. They felt very important. This was a REAL mystery now, not a silly made-up one—and they were in it!

"Right—you go straight away," said Nicky, pleased to think that the girls would not be able to track them up the hill, and follow them to the tower, as he had been half afraid they would. They would be safe in the museum. He stood up. "I'll go and get lunch-packets for the two of us, Ken," he said. "Mrs. Hawes will make some— she'll give us smashing sandwiches! And I'll take a bone and some biscuits for old Punch. That be all right for you, Punch, old chap?"

Punch danced round him, delighted to hear Nicky talking to him at last.

"Wuff, wuff!" he said, and Nicky patted him. Punch ran to Penny, and she patted him too. "You'd better not ask *Winnie* for a pat," she said. "She hasn't forgotten how you tried to drown her shoe yesterday!"

At the word "shoe" Punch was off like lightning. Nicky groaned. "*Why* did you mention the word 'shoe'? I thought he'd forgotten all about shoes to-day—he hasn't dragged any downstairs at all. Now he's gone to fetch some, I bet you anything you like!"

He and Ken went back through the hedge to find Mrs. Hawes, who was very pleased to make them sandwiches.

"That dog of yours shot past me at sixty miles

an hour just now," she said. " Up to some kind of mischief, I expect ! "

And, sure enough, by the time the boys were ready to go, and the neat packets of sandwiches were on the kitchen table, Punch had raided all the bedrooms, and brought at least six pairs of shoes into the kitchen !

" You take them back ! " ordered Mrs. Hawes, pointing at them with the bread-knife. " If you think *I'm* going to trot up and down the stairs with all those shoes, you'd better think again ! "

" Oh you *ass*, Punch ! " said Nicky, gathering them up. " This trick isn't funny any more ! Ken, take the packets of sandwiches and stick them into my shoulder-bag, will you ? And fetch some apples and bananas from the side-board, and take a couple of ginger-beers from the larder. I'll bring some chocolate—and biscuits and bone for Punch—though he jolly well doesn't deserve them, messing about with everyone's shoes like this ! "

Mrs. Hawes heaved a sigh of relief when all three were safely out of the house, Punch barking his head off with joy. He was off for the day with the boys—could anything be more exciting than that ? Ah well, Punch—it may perhaps be a little more exciting than any of you imagine !

CHAPTER 14

THE CELLARS IN THE HILL

WHILE THE two boys set off to go up Skylark Hill, Penny and Winnie walked in the opposite direction to the little local museum.

" There's Harriet's sister, look," said Penny, nodding towards a plump little woman who was dusting the glass-fronted museum cases. " Hallo, Miss Clewes! How's Harriet? I haven't seen her to-day."

"She's in bed with a cold, miss," said Miss Clewes. "Well, it's not often I see *you* here—last time I saw you was when you came with your school class to see some old documents about our village. What do you want to see this morning?"

"Well, Miss Clewes, we're rather interested in that great old place up on Skylark Hill," said Penny. "The one that was burnt down years ago. Are there any maps of it?"

"Oh, yes—plenty!" said Miss Clewes, bustling over to a cupboard. "Funny you should come about that old place—there's been quite a lot of people looking at the old plans lately. But surely nobody would want to build that awful old building up again, would they?"

"What sort of people came?" asked Penny, surprised.

"Well—not very *nice* folks, miss," said Miss Clewes, getting some enormous stiff papers out of a cupboard. "Men, you know—off-hand like—almost rude—poring over them plans, and making notes. I says to them, "What's all the excitement about, all of a sudden? Thinking of re-building the old place and living there in style, like in the old days?""

"And what did they say to that?" asked Penny.

"Oh, they said maybe they *were* going to do that, and maybe they *weren't*," said little Miss Clewes.

" And that it wasn't none of *my* business ! Quite rude, they were."

Penny and Winnie unrolled the enormous plans and studied them. They were not very clever at making out what the plans showed. They ignored the ones of the great house itself, because the fire had destroyed all the rooms, both upstairs and down, and only the stone walls were standing now.

" Are these the plans of the cellars ? " asked Winnie, poring over a curious map that showed what looked like passages and caves.

" Yes—the plans of the house itself aren't much use to anyone now it's burnt," said Miss Clewes, " but the plans of the passages and caves that honeycomb the hill are still more or less correct, I should think. The folk who used to live in the old place used them as cellars—but they were *natural* cellars, if you know what I mean—not man-made. Saved them the trouble of digging out cellars for the goods or the food they wanted to store ! "

" Are there any old stories—old legends about the place ? " asked Winnie.

" Well—a few—but I wouldn't put much belief in them," said Miss Clewes, rolling up the plans the girls had finished with. " There's the story about the Golden Statue, for instance. They do say it's got magic powers, and if its feet are kissed seven times, it will grant wishes."

" A nice story—but I'm afraid no statue could grant wishes ! " said Penny. " Not even a golden one. What happened when the place was burnt down ? Did the statue melt and disappear ? It must have been worth a lot of money."

" Nobody knows what happened to it," said Miss Clewes. " I suppose it *might* have melted, the heat was so great. Or it might have been removed to safety, and taken by the family to wherever they went. Or it *might* be just a story, you know—all kinds of tales grow up about old places."

" Yes, that's true," said Penny. " Do you mind if I quickly trace the plan of the old passages and caves in the hill just near the burnt building—the ones used as cellars ? We might go exploring there to-day."

" No—now don't you do that," said Miss Clewes. " Since we had a great storm and a cloud-burst of rain five years since, those underground places have been dangerous—fallen in, you know, or full of water. You'd much better not go exploring there."

" Well, we'll see," said Penny, putting a piece of tracing paper over the map, and running her pencil here and there. " I'll let you know what happens if we *do* explore ! "

The girls left the museum at last, taking with them a very well-traced copy of the passages and caves that made up the "Cellars" of the old building.

"I don't expect it will be of any use," said Penny. "But you never know! It wouldn't *really* matter if the boys got lost in the cellars, because Punch could easily take them out. A dog always knows the way! What shall we do now?"

"Well, I'm jolly hungry," said Winnie. "Let's go home, and get some sandwiches and apples, and go up on Skylark Hill. I know the boys don't want us spying on them, but we could just have a look round. We could sit and have our sandwiches on the hill, and hear the birds singing—especially the skylarks, of course!"

So back they went and made themselves some ham sandwiches, and took some apples from the larder. Then they set off to Skylark Hill and found a cosy place at the bottom, where they could sit and munch in peace.

"Let's have a good look at our map-tracing, too," said Penny. "I've an idea it might help us a lot. If only we could find the lower entrance to the cellars! That would save us going all the way up to the old building!"

It was very pleasant sitting in the sun, munching, and poring over the map. Penny rolled it up at last. "I wonder what the boys have been doing," she said. "How I'd like to know! Well—let's have a walk up the hill, and see if we can spot anything interesting. My word, we have been a time eating our lunch ! "

The boys had had a most adventurous time. They had gone up to the old tower first of all, and examined it thoroughly, trying to find some traces of whoever had been signalling there the night before.

" Here's another match like the one we found before," announced Ken, picking one up from the stone sill. " This is the window-opening that the signaller must have used last night. And here's a second match on the floor—*and* a cigarette packet —empty ! All clues, Nicky ! I'll put them in my pocket."

" Well, at least we know some *real* person was here," said Nicky. " It wasn't just a ghost signalling ! "

They made their way down the dangerous stairway, and Ken picked up yet another match—and then, down in the great old kitchen, they found an empty matchbox, thrown near the old iron stoves. They looked at the name on the matchbox.

" Ha—the signaller uses Quick-Lite Matches ! " said Ken. " And we know he smokes Splendour Cigarettes, because he left the empty packet behind. He's not very careful, is he ? "

" Why should he be ? " said Nicky. " He's probably only using this place to signal from, because from here any flash can be seen for miles —and he's away long before daylight, I should think."

" He could hide quite well in those old cellars," suggested Ken.

" Maybe. Yes—that's quite a thought. Or somebody might be using them as a hiding-place for goods of some sort—and perhaps the time has come for whatever's hidden to be fetched in safety. You know, I think we've hit on something ! "

" You mean valuables may have been stored away in those old caves and passages—maybe stolen some time ago—and the robbers arranged for a signal to be given when it was safe for the stolen goods to be fetched. A signal from someone in the know ? "

" Yes—something like that," said Nicky, feeling suddenly very excited. " Gosh, this is thrilling ! We certainly MUST go and explore those cellars. Thank goodness we've brought strong torches— and Punch. He'll bark like anything if there's anyone down there."

" Perhaps that's why he barked the other day ? " said Ken. " Maybe there was someone down here then."

" Yes. I say—isn't this getting EXCITING !

What about going down now? There's nothing
more to be seen here. I've got the matches—and
the cigarette packet. Come on—we'll go down the
cellar stairs very quietly, and tell Punch not even
to growl!"

So once again the boys went underground down
the curious spiral stairway, into pitch darkness,
Punch at their heels. Nicky flashed his torch
cautiously around. They were in the same dark,
low-roofed passage they had found themselves in
the day before. They went quietly down it and
came to the cellar they had seen heaped with old
junk. That was as far as they had gone yesterday,
for it was here that Nicky's battery had given out,
and they had been forced to go back.

But now their torches shone steadily and brilliantly before them, making a path through the
darkness. They stood listening, and Nicky put
his hand on Punch's collar to stop him running
forward. Not a sound could be heard, and Punch
gave a very small whine. He wanted to go on!

"All right, Punch—but go quietly and carefully,"
Nicky warned him. "We don't know what's down
here—nor do we know who may be hiding—so walk
just in front of us, see?"

They went silently through another passage
whose roof became so low at one part that the boys
had to bend double to get through. Punch was

very good. He stopped whenever they did, walked very slowly, and kept his nose in the air, sniffing for smells of animals or humans, all the time.

They came to three caves, all running into one another, and then another passage, a wide one this time. And then, what a surprise—they came to a cave piled with tins, boxes and cartons of all sorts and sizes! Nicky shone his torch on them.

"Tins of meat—butter—bacon—cartons of cigarettes—packets—gracious, what's all this?" he whispered. "Someone's been living here for some time—look at all the empty tins and cartons—as well as all the unopened ones. This must be where that signaller lives!"

"Better go carefully then," whispered Ken. "He may be near."

They went down another passage, so narrow that it was hard at times to squeeze through. And then Punch stood absolutely still and gave a very small, deep growl!

The two boys hardly dared to breathe. What was Punch growling at? Then they knew! A long-drawn-out snore came to their ears—and then another! SOMEONE was there—someone fast asleep. Who was it? Be careful now, Nicky and Ken—this may be a very dangerous moment!

CHAPTER 15

DEEP UNDERGROUND

THE TWO BOYS stood perfectly still, Punch just in front of them, still growling softly.

" Sh ! " whispered Nicky, and Punch stopped growling at once. " Take hold of Punch's collar, Ken, while I go forward a little."

Ken held Punch's collar tightly while Nicky went cautiously forward. The passage curved just there, and Nicky felt sure the snorer was just round the bend. He put his head round—and there, in a little side-cave, was an enormous man, lying on his back, snoring. Beside him were the remains of a meal, taken out of tins.

Nicky stared at him. He was dark-skinned and wore a fine beard. Nicky thought he looked as if he came from the East—was he an Indian—or perhaps a Persian? He looked pretty fierce, anyway! What on earth was he doing in the underground cellars?

Then Nicky saw tools of all kinds—spades big and small—iron bars—buckets! He was astonished. Were the men excavating, then—digging out the caves—were they looking for something?

He crept back to Ken, and pulled him farther up the passage, so as to be out of the sleeping man's hearing, should he awake.

"Something's certainly going on down in these old cellars," he said. "There are all kinds of digging tools down there—and a big, foreign-looking man with a beard is snoring away near them! What is he digging for? Who would hide anything in these caves?"

"I don't know," said Ken, puzzled. "Maybe precious things were stored here when that great old building was lived in—or taken down here for safety when the fire began, and hidden—and then perhaps forgotten."

" Or they might have been *stolen* when the fire raged," said Nicky. " Maybe someone fired the old place on purpose, so that they could run off with some of the really valuable things. After all, it was a Prince who built that place—he must have been very rich and had some wonderful treasures."

" Yes—an Eastern Prince," said Ken. " You said that snoring fellow down there looks foreign ? I bet it's someone who's been told where something is hidden—hidden in this hill."

" Goodness—that's just like we put in our coded message ! " said Nicky, startled. " Don't you remember—we put, ' Stuff hidden on Skylark Hill ' ! Little did we know how true that was ! "

" And we put in about the signalling from the tower, too," said Ken. " That came true, as well ! What was the other thing we put ? Oh yes— ' Meet in cellars ' ! Gosh, it looks as if that's correct, too. I say—it's all a bit queer, isn't it ? "

" It is rather," said Nicky. " I mean—we only thought of our silly message just as a joke—something to amuse Uncle Bob. I don't much like the way it's all coming true. It's just as if we'd foretold what was going to happen."

" Well—we can't stop it now," said Ken. " We'd better look out for this Cellar Meeting next! Perhaps someone is coming to talk to that snoring fellow. We might overhear something interesting."

Punch began to growl again, and Nicky tapped his head. "Shut up! No noise now, Punch. Someone else may be coming."

Nicky was right! The boys suddenly heard a scraping noise as if someone was coming up a passage to where the snoring man lay in the little side-cave. Then a man's voice spoke angrily.

"Hassan! Always you sleep! Why are you not working? Have you dug out the golden urns?"

The sleeping man had awakened with a jump. He growled something in a language that the boys did not understand. Then there came the sound of metal rubbing against metal, and the boys imagined that Hassan was showing the other man what he had dug out.

"Did you find the statue?" asked the visitor.

Apparently Hassan answered no, for the second man flew into a rage, and shouted a string of words that the boys couldn't understand. Punch couldn't help growling when he heard the angry shouts.

His growl must have been heard, for the two men suddenly fell silent.

"What was that?" said the second man, in English. "Could it be Harry coming down from the passages above? He was in the tower last night, signalling for the others to meet him here, and take the stuff."

Ken gave Nicky a sudden nudge. *Harry!* Good gracious, that was the name Ken had chosen when he had signed that secret message! This was really very weird. Harry! He must be the head of this gang. Would he come?

"Hope he won't come down this way," whispered Ken. "We'd be caught then, between Harry and the others. Golly—I don't much like this!"

He fell silent—and in the silence the two boys heard another noise. Someone *was* coming down from the old building above—coming down by the very same path that they themselves had taken. The boys hurriedly squeezed into a little side-cave, pulling Punch with them. If only this fellow would go by without seeing them!

He would have done, but for Punch, who simply could *not* resist another growl—rather a loud one this time. The man stopped at once.

"What's that? Who's there?" he called, roughly.

There was no answer, of course—and then, alas, Punch growled again, a deep, angry growl that rumbled all round the little cave. The man bent down and looked into the cave. He was an ugly fellow, with a black shade over one eye. He flashed a torch on the boys and the dog.

"What's this? Who are you? What on earth are you doing here?" he shouted. Then he yelled to the other two men, who were looking extremely startled. "Look! There's a couple of kids here! Didn't I tell you to keep watch, and see that no one came down here? You idiots! Just when everything's almost ready! We've only got that statue to find now! I'll knock your heads together —didn't I TELL you that . . ."

"It's all right, Harry," said the second man. "If it's only kids we can shut them up in a cave, and put a stone in front of it. We'll soon be out of here—by to-morrow at the latest."

"To-morrow will be too late," shouted Harry. "Someone may come hunting for these two kids —just when we want to take out all the stuff. We'd better go and tell the other two men to come up and help to-night."

He turned to the two frightened boys. "Well, you've got mixed up in something you didn't expect," he said, in a voice the boys didn't like at all. "Well—we shan't hurt you—but you'll just have to stay imprisoned in a cave till we're ready to go. Come on out of there—we'll find another cave for you with an entrance we can easily block."

The boys made no move, and the man lost his

temper. He dragged them both out roughly—
and Punch went completely mad. He flew at the
man and bit him hard on the left foot, right through
his shoe! The man gave an anguished yell, and
pulled off his shoe at once. His foot was bleeding
through his thin sock.

The other two men came running up and one of
them aimed a vicious kick at poor Punch. How he
yelped! He ran to Nicky at once, but he ran on
three legs, because one of his hind legs was badly
hurt by the kick. Nicky picked him up and ran,
Ken close behind him.

The men stumbled after them. " Look—let's get
into that narrow passage running off to the left—
the roof's so low that I don't think the men will
be able to squeeze through after us," panted Nicky.

" Right," said Ken, and he squeezed in after
Nicky, who found it very difficult with Punch in
his arms. In fact he had to put him down at the
end of the narrow passage, because there he had
to crawl on hands and knees, the roof was so low!

The men stopped—and one of them laughed.
" Couldn't be better! They'll be nicely boxed up
in there. We only need to roll up a heavy stone,
and they'll be imprisoned! Serve them right—
and that dog, too! "

The boys heard the sound of the men tugging
at a stone—and then—thud—it was right up against

the opening to the narrow passage, completely blocking it.

But neither of the boys worried about that. It was poor, whining Punch they were upset about. They shone a torch on to his leg, fearing that it was broken.

Thank goodness it wasn't—although it was badly bruised and bleeding. Nicky hugged Punch lovingly.

" You brave little dog ! " he said. " I'm *glad* you bit that man. Does your leg hurt very much ? Poor old Punch—where's my hanky ? I'll bind up your leg, and hope it will be all right."

Punch licked him, and gave a tiny whine as if to say, " Don't worry ! We'll be all right ! " But *would* they be all right ? Did the men *really* mean to leave them imprisoned ? And if so, how in the world would anyone ever find them ?

CHAPTER 16

THE TWO BOYS sat silently for a while, with their arms round Punch. How sickening to be caught like this! Then Ken remembered the food they had brought with them in the bag. He brightened up at once.

" Let's have something to eat," he said. " It's about dinner-time, and I bet Punch would like his bone! Sandwiches will cheer us up! "

They certainly did! After the boys had eaten half the sandwiches, they felt very much better. They had a banana each too, and Punch had a biscuit. Then they drank one of the bottles of ginger-beer.

" Better not eat everything now," said Ken. " You just never know how long we'll be imprisoned here."

" *Not* a very nice thought," said Nicky. " Well, anyway the girls know we've come up here, so if we don't appear for some time, they'll tell Dad, and he'll organise a search-party. Wait, though —what about trying to move that stone away that they've put at the entrance of this place? We *might* be able to."

They crawled down the passage to the entrance. It was well and truly blocked with a very heavy stone indeed. No amount of shoving would move it. Punch came along and looked, too. He began to scrape round the stone with his front paws, and managed to make a small space between the stone and the rocky entrance.

But, alas, it wasn't nearly big enough for either of the boys to squeeze through, try as they would. However, Punch managed to wriggle out, and set off cautiously on three legs down the passage where the men had gone.

" Be careful, Punch ! " called Nicky. " Come back before you get into any more trouble." Punch went on very cautiously, giving a little growl every now and again. If only he could find those men, what a fright he would give them !

He came to the cave where Hassan, the sleeping man, had been. No one was there. Punch sniffed round and came across one odd shoe. It was the shoe that Harry had removed from his swollen, bleeding foot, and thrown down in the cave when he limped away to help the others in their work of shifting some goods.

A shoe ! Ah—Punch simply couldn't resist picking it up in his mouth and running off with it !

Back he went to the boys' cave, shoe in mouth, proud of himself. Why, even down here he could show off his latest trick!

The boys couldn't help laughing when they saw Punch with the shoe in his mouth!

"Punch, you dear old idiot!" said Nicky. "Where did you get that? Oh, of course—it must be the shoe that fellow took off when you bit his foot. Put it down, old thing—he can jolly well go without it!"

"I say, Nicky—do you suppose we could get out of the *other* end of this cave?" Ken suddenly said, shining his torch towards the back. "There must have been a fall of earth at some time—so if we dig through with our hands, we may find a passage we can go up."

"Right. Let's try," said Nicky, bored with doing nothing. So he and Ken and Punch all dug hard with hands and paws. The earth was very loose, and it was soon obvious that part of the earthy roof *had* fallen in and blocked the passage.

"We're through the fall of earth!" said Ken, suddenly, as his hand went through the last layer of soil into nothing. "Quick—we'll soon have a hole big enough for us to squeeze through. Gracious—old Punch is through already. What's the other side, Punch?"

Punch began to growl. He was on the other side of the earth-fall, and the boys could not see what he was growling at.

" There surely can't be any of the men there ! " said Ken. " Here, let *me* wriggle through the hole we've made and shine my torch to see what's the other side. Punch must be growling at *something* ! "

So Ken wriggled a little more, and was then able to shine his torch into the space beyond. He was silent for so long that Nicky grew impatient.

" What is it ? Can you see something ? "

" Yes. Yes, I can certainly see something. But I can't believe it ! " said Ken, in an awed voice. " Nicky—get beside me and look. I must be seeing things ! It's—it's so strange ! "

Nicky squeezed beside him and looked into the dark space lighted by Ken's torch. He caught his breath in wonder and fear. Something very beautiful was there—something that looked at them out of brilliantly shining eyes, and shone brightly from top to toe.

" What is it ? " whispered Nicky.

" Well—can it be the statue that one of the men spoke about ? " Ken whispered back. " Nicky— it's made of *gold*—pure, shining *gold*. And its eyes are precious stones. It's a statue from one of the far Eastern lands—it must have belonged to the prince who built that burnt-out mansion. Someone must have taken it down here for safety when the fire started."

"And stuffed it right at the back of the cave— and then a fall of earth came, and it was hidden from everyone's sight!" said Nicky. "No one has found it since! We heard the men talking about finding golden urns—you remember—they must have been hidden down here, too. And after all these years *somebody* has remembered them, and sent men here to look for them!"

"But that *statue*! Did you ever see anything like it?" said Ken, shining his torch on the strangely beautiful face. "I say—we mustn't let the men know it's here!"

"They're too big to get through that narrow low tunnel to it," said Nicky. "We could only just squeeze through it ourselves. This is *our* secret, Ken! My word—it's a wonder we didn't put a statue into our coded message, isn't it?"

"I do wish we could get out of here," said Ken. "There's rock behind that statue, so the passage must end there. Let's get back into the other part—there's more room. My *word*—what a find! And to think it was all by accident that we spotted it! Come back, Punch—look, Nicky, he's licking the statue's feet to see what it's made of! It's gold, Punch, gold!"

"What do you suppose the girls are doing?" said Nicky, when they were back through the hole they had made, sitting in the cave again. "I wish I knew where they were!"

At that very moment Penny and Winnie were walking up Skylark Hill, excited because they had such a good tracing of the underground cellars in their hands. They were about half-way up when Penny stopped.

"Look—there's a queer-looking man coming down the hill!" she said. "Foreign-looking—see his very black beard. Isn't he tall!"

"And look at the man with the black eye-shade," said Winnie. "He's limping! He's wearing only one shoe, and see, his foot's bleeding! And there's another man behind him. Where in the world can they have come from? They appeared so *very* suddenly!"

"Winnie—do you think they've come from the underground cellars?" said Penny, suddenly. "You know how far down the hill they stretch—and we do know there's an entrance at this lower end, as well as through the kitchen of the old place—and you remember that the boys told us that Punch must have found a way out, too? Well—*I* think those men have come from the same outlet Punch found, when the boys missed him the other day.

There's simply nowhere else on this hill for them to have so suddenly appeared from ! "

" Look—I think that one-eyed man is coming up to us," said Winnie, in a fright.

Sure enough the man with the eye-shade came right up and spoke to them.

" I need a doctor," he said. " My foot is bad. It has been bitten by a dog. Can you tell me of a doctor, please ? "

" Er—well—there's one down in the town there," stammered Penny, frightened, pointing down the hill. " Anyone will tell you where he lives. Er—what kind of a dog bit you ? "

The man didn't answer, but went back to the others, limping. They set off down the hill again.

" I *bet* it was Punch who bit him ! " said Winnie. " I bet it was. Oh, Penny—you don't think anything's happened to the boys, do you ? Hadn't we better go back home for help ? "

" No—we'll try to find the place where the men came out of the hill," said Penny. " I feel as if we ought to look for the boys and make sure they're all right. Come on—this way. That's where we first saw the men appear, over there. Hurry, Winnie—the men may come back at any time."

There they go, the two of them, anxious and scared. There must be some way in, there must !

CHAPTER 17

THE GIRLS ARE VERY CLEVER

PENNY and Winnie made their way round the slope of the hill to where they had first seen the men appearing. They kept looking back over their shoulders to make sure that no one was following them.

" This is quite an adventure, Penny, isn't it ? " said Winnie, in rather a trembly voice. Then she gave a loud exclamation. " OH! I *say*—I've thought of something."

" You made me jump ! " said Penny, who was feeling just as scared as Winnie. " What have you thought of ? "

" That tracing we made of the underground cellars ! " said Winnie. " Let's have a look at it, and see if it will help us."

They sat down on the hillside and opened out the roll of tracing paper. They pored over it, frowning.

" Here's the old building, see," said Penny, her finger on the map. " And here's where the cellars begin. They go along here—down under the hill,

They pored over it, frowning.

of course—and spread out here and there—really underground passages, I suppose. But I don't see how we're going to tell where they *end* on this actual hill."

"Look—what's this on the tracing?" said Winnie, pointing to a little curving line. "Could it be a stream?"

"Well, I suppose it might," said Penny. "But what's the use of that? There's no stream here on the hill now, that I can see. It must have dried up years ago."

"But its *bed* will still be there—like a dried-up ditch!" said Winnie, jumping up. "Come on— if we can find that, and follow it up, we shall perhaps come across the bottom entrance to the cellars!"

The girls walked over to the place where they had first seen the three men appearing. They looked all round but at first saw nothing that could have been a stream-bed. Then Winnie gave a shout.

"Here you are! This must have once been a stream—the ditch running along this old hawthorn hedge."

"Yes—I think you're right," said Penny, excited. She looked at the traced map again. "Here it is on the map," she said. "And look—it seems to go curving up the hill, and swings off just by where the entrance to the cellars is marked. Let's follow it up the hill."

So the two girls went slowly up the hill, following the half-lost track of the old stream. But where could the entrance into the hill be found?

The old ditch took a sudden curve round—and Penny gave an exclamation.

" The entrance should be here—where the ditch curves—look on the map and see what I mean, Winnie. This is where we must hunt for the entrance, I'm sure!"

She was right. A great gorse bush barred their way, thick and prickly. The ditch curved round it —and Penny's quick eye saw a smooth patch of earth just under one side of the great bush.

"·I think *that's* the way into the opening," she said. " See that worn patch of earth? The men may have gone in and out there. Good gracious —we shall be scratched to bits!"

They certainly did get well and truly scratched! Fortunately they both had coats, and were able to wrap them round their faces and shoulders as they crawled under the prickly bush. Someone had cut away the bush in the thick middle part, so it was not so thorny there—and what a surprise they had!

A hole went down into the ground, almost under the middle of the bush—a hole that had rough steps cut in one side! The girls crouched under

the bush, and looked down into the hole rather doubtfully.

"Do we go down?" said Penny. "We don't know what's down there—or who."

"Oh, come on—let's be brave!" said Winnie, who was not feeling brave in the least. "I'll go first."

And down she went, groping with her legs to find the rough steps. Soon she was in an underground passage. She switched on the torch she had brought.

"Well—that was very clever of us," said Penny,

jumping down and joining her. " Now—where do we go from here ? "

" Well—there's only one way—and that's *up*," said Winnie. " Thank goodness you took that tracing, Penny. Come on—I'll go first."

The two girls went slowly up the dark passage. They flashed their torches into little and big side-caves, marvelling at seeing so many. What a honeycombed hillside this was. There must have been many little underground streams at one time, rushing down to make such a number of caves and passages !

" Shall we shout and see if the boys answer ? " said Penny. " There doesn't seem to be anyone here—no men, I mean. Let's shout."

So they shouted at the tops of their voices. " KEN ! NICKY ! PUNCH ! "

The two boys were still far away from the girls, sitting in their tiny cave, and heard nothing. But Punch's ears were very sharp. He cocked them up and listened. What was that far-off noise ? He growled.

" Oh, *don't* say the men are coming again," groaned Nicky. " I'm fed up with them. What's the matter, Punch ? "

Punch heard the far-away voices once more, and stood up on three legs, holding up his hurt one. He didn't growl this time. Surely he recognised those voices! He put his head on one side and listened hard.

The girls shouted again as they came up the underground passages in the hillside—and this time Punch knew the voices. Why—that was Penny's voice—and that was Winnie's! WUFF-WUFF-WUFF!

Punch barked loudly and joyfully, almost deafening the two boys in that small place. They stared at him in astonishment.

"What's the matter, Punch, old thing?" said Nicky. "You're barking *happily*—who's coming? It can't be the men or you'd be growling."

Punch gave Nicky a quick lick and then barked again. He could hear the girls coming nearer and nearer. They heard his bark, and knew they were near the boys. "We're coming, Nicky, we're coming, Ken. Where are you?" they yelled.

"Here! Here! Can you hear us?" shouted Nicky in delight, crawling as near as he could to the great stone that blocked the entrance. "Penny! Winnie! Here we are—imprisoned in this cave."

The girls at last came to where the boys were, and yelled to them.

"We're here! We came all the way up from the lower entrance—the one Punch must have found the other day. We saw the men—they spoke to us!"

"Gosh! Did they *see* you coming up here?"

asked Nicky, as the two girls began to try and move the great stone from the entrance.

"No—they've gone down to the town to find a doctor!" shouted Winnie. "I hope it was Punch who bit that man with the black eye-shade."

"It was," answered Ken. "Look—we'll *push* this stone while you *pull*. It's such a weight that I doubt if even the four of us can move it."

To their enormous disappointment the great stone could not be moved even an inch! It had taken three strong men to put it there—and four children certainly would not be able to budge it. It was most disappointing.

Punch barked, and scrabbled frantically with his front paws, but it was no use. Everyone sat back to take a rest, and the boys told the girls about the wonderful golden statue they had discovered in the hole behind their cave.

"*Gracious!* Miss Clewes at the museum told us about that!" said Penny. "It's quite a legend, she said. And apparently anyone who wants a wish to come true has only to kiss the statue's feet seven times!"

"Well, *I'm* not going to kiss any statue's feet, not even to get free," said Nicky. "Gosh—what are we to do *now*? I don't like you girls hanging about in these passages in case those men come back. They'd make *you* prisoners too!"

" Would they ? " said Winnie, in alarm. " Then hadn't we better go back straight away and get help ? We could bring your Uncle Bob up here in no time, and your father, too ! "

" Yes—I almost think you'd better do that," said Ken. " Don't you agree, Nicky ? But I *bet* Uncle Bob won't believe you girls ! Gosh, this mystery has come true in every detail in a most remarkable way ! I'm never going to make up any more ! "

" We'll go now," said Penny. " Cheer up, both of you—and pat old Punch for us. We'll be as quick as ever we can ! "

And away went the two girls, very cautiously indeed. The boys sat silent, listening to the small noises made by the girls as they went down the passage. Punch listened, too, his head on one side.

" Can't hear them any more," said Ken, with a sigh. " I'm getting tired of this hole, aren't you, Nicky ? Well—I just hope the men don't come back. I say—what do you suppose Uncle Bob will say when we show him the golden statue ? "

" Oh—he simply won't believe it ! " said Nicky, with a grin. " It's just part of the Mystery that Never Was. He—just—won't—believe it ! "

CHAPTER 18

UNCLE BOB TO THE RESCUE!

THE TWO GIRLS went down the dark passage, their ears open for any sound of the men coming back again. Penny thought she heard a noise and stopped in alarm.

" Do you think it would be wiser to go *up* the passages to the old kitchen, and get out that way —the way the boys told us about ? " said Penny. " It would be so terrifying if we met the men."

" No. Let's go on down," said Winnie. " At least we *know* this way. The men won't be back yet. I expect they've not only gone to find a doctor but also to make plans for removing whatever they have found in the old caves. I *am* glad that Punch bit one of them ! "

They came safely to the opening under the old gorse bush. It seemed to be more difficult getting out than getting in, and the girls were in a very dirty, untidy state when at last they were safely out of the great bush, and standing on the hillside in the sun.

" My word—it's good to be out in the open air

and sunshine again!" said Penny, breathing in deeply. "I'm sorry for the two boys, shut up in that horrid little cave. Buck up—let's get back as soon as ever we can, and tell everyone where the boys are. Nicky's father is home to-day, isn't he? He can help too, and Nicky's Uncle Bob and . . ."

"I wonder if his Uncle Bob will believe our story," said Winnie. "It does sound a bit peculiar, doesn't it—hidden men—caves—a golden statue— the boys made prisoners. Still, strange things *do* happen—you see them in the papers every day."

"Well, I never thought an adventure like this would happen to *us*!" said Penny. "Usually adventures are things that happen to other people. Come on—we're nearly home."

"I've been looking out for those men all the way back, but there hasn't been a sign of them," said Winnie. "I'd run for miles if I did meet them!"

"We're back at last!" said Penny, as they came to Nicky's front gate. She ran into the house, calling for Nicky's mother and father. "Mr. Fraser! Mrs. Fraser! Are you in? Quick!"

"Nicky's Dad has gone to the bank, and his Mother's gone shopping, miss!" called Mrs. Hawes from the kitchen. "But his Uncle's in the garden reading the paper, if you want him."

"Yes, we *do*!" said Penny, and flew out into

It seemed to be more difficult getting out . . . .

the garden, with Winnie close behind. " Uncle Bob! UNCLE BOB!"

" Hallo, hallo — what's all the excitement for, Penny? " said Uncle Bob, in surprise. " And where are the boys this morning? "

" Uncle Bob, something's happened," panted Penny. " The boys went up to the old burnt building this morning to find out about that signalling, and . . ."

" Now listen—I don't want to hear any more fairy tales," said Uncle Bob, looking annoyed. " I'm TIRED of hearing what's in that silly message, I'm TIRED of the boys pretending that something's going on. The joke's OVER!"

" But Uncle Bob—the boys are prisoners in a horrid little cave," said Penny, almost in tears. " A cave with a beautiful golden statue at the end . . ."

" And if you kiss its feet and wish, your wish comes true!" said Winnie.

Uncle Bob threw down his paper in exasperation. " What next! Do you *really* expect me to believe in a golden statue that grants wishes? You must be mad. Go away."

" The men have pushed a great heavy stone in front of the boys' cave," said Penny, in a suddenly trembling voice. " And Punch is hurt. One of the men kicked him. Oh, where's Nicky's father? I

MUST get someone to help Nicky and Ken. We saw those horrible men walking down the hillside, but I'm sure they'll soon be back. Winnie, let's go and find *my* Daddy. He'll tell the police, I'm sure he will."

Tears suddenly ran down her cheeks, and Uncle Bob looked at her in surprise. He took her hand. "Penny—listen to me—are you *really* telling the truth? This isn't just another idiotic bit of made-up mystery, is it? You remember the silly coded message I showed you, and told you of—about a meeting in cellars—and stuff hidden on Skylark Hill—and signals from the tower—signed Harry—that the boys made up between them? Well, are you *sure* this isn't another silly bit of nonsense?"

"It wasn't nonsense—it's all *true*!" wept Penny. "It *came* true, I don't know how, but it *did*. And 'Harry' is one of the men; Uncle Bob, if you won't come and help, I'll *have* to go and find Daddy."

"Well—this is about the queerest thing I've ever come across," said Uncle Bob. "How *could* a made-up mystery have any truth in it? All right, all right, I'm coming, Penny. Stop crying. I believe you, dear, though I'm blessed if I understand what's happening. Come along—we'll all go back to Skylark Hill."

So, much to the girls' relief, Uncle Bob hurried off with them to Skylark Hill. The birds were singing there, just as they had been on the morning he had been there before, but none of them stayed to listen. The girls were anxious to get back to the boys before the men returned—and Uncle Bob was beginning to feel not only puzzled, but most disturbed. What in the world was going on?

The girls took him to the great gorse bush. " The entrance is right in the middle—there's a hole that goes underground," said Penny. " I saw the men coming from somewhere about here—and Winnie and I looked at a map we have, and it showed an entrance just about here, too—so we hunted till we found it. It's awfully prickly, Uncle Bob."

" Bless us all—what next ! " said Uncle Bob, not at all liking the idea of creeping under the great thorny bush, and sliding down underground. " My word—I haven't brought a torch ! "

" It's all right—we've one each," said Winnie. " Do hurry—I'm so afraid the men will be back. And they're HORRID, Uncle Bob ! "

With many groans, Uncle Bob managed to get down the steps that led into the passage below. The girls switched on their torches, and at once beams of light cut through the darkness.

" This way," said Penny. " We can only go uphill. We pass lots of caves on the way."

Uncle Bob followed the two girls, wondering if he was dreaming! He saw the cave where the tools lay scattered about—he saw the hoard of tins, some opened and empty, some still untouched. And then, in the distance, he heard a noise. He stopped.

"Wait—what's that?" he said.

"It's all right—it's only Punch barking," said Penny. "We'll soon come to the cave where the boys are. Who would have thought that the hill was honeycombed with passages and caves like this, Uncle Bob?"

As soon as Punch began to bark the boys wondered who was coming. Was it the men again? Surely it couldn't be the girls back with help already?

"Wuff-wuff-wuff-wuff!" barked Punch madly, scraping with his paws at the big stone blocking the cave entrance. *He* knew who was coming— he knew those voices as soon as he heard them far away in the distance!

"Here's the cave—and there's the stone the men put in front, that we can't move," said Penny. "NICKY! KEN! We're here, and Uncle Bob's with us! You shove the stone and we'll tug it."

"Hallo, Uncle!" shouted Nicky, in delight. "Come on, now—all together!" And he and Ken shoved at the great stone with all their might, while Uncle tugged and pulled till he was out of breath. The stone moved!

"It's coming!" yelled Penny, doing her bit, too. "Shove again, boys! It's moving!"

The stone gave way so suddenly that the girls and Uncle Bob fell over. The boys crawled out at once, with Punch barking loudly, leaping round on three legs!

"WELL!" said Uncle Bob, sitting on the ground, rubbing his grazed hands, for the stone was very rough and hard. "This *is* a do, isn't it! I could hardly believe the story that the girls came and told me. And what's all this about a golden statue?"

"Crawl into this cave, and you'll see a fall of earth near the end of it," said Nicky. "Poke my torch through the hole in the middle of the fall, and see what's beyond!"

Uncle Bob did as he was told, though with much difficulty—and when he saw the gleaming beauty of the magnificent golden statue, he was so amazed that at first he couldn't say a word.

"Well—what do you think about our pretend-mystery *now*?" said Nicky, triumphantly. "We didn't put a golden statue in it—but everything else has come true!"

"I certainly have an apology to make to you all," said Uncle Bob, wriggling out of the cave.

" This is a most extraordinary find. I must get on to the police AT ONCE ! Come along—let's get back to the town. We oughtn't to lose any time— those men may come back for the other things they found, though probably not till night-time."

Excited, chattering, thrilled to the core, the little party began to make its way down to the great gorse bush. They clambered up the hole one by one, and squeezed through the opening, pricked once more by the bush that guarded it.

And what should they see, as soon as they came into the open, but the three men straggling back up the hill ! Harry had his foot bound up now, and was walking with a limp.

" There they are ! " yelled Nicky. " LOOK ! "

At his shout the men stopped in surprise—then turned tail and made off, Harry limping painfully down the hill. The boys were too stiff to go after them, and the girls too scared. Uncle Bob grabbed hold of Nicky in case he *should* take it into his head to chase them ! Punch limped down the hill on three legs, barking, but soon came back.

" Let them go," said Uncle Bob. " The police will soon round them up ! You've had enough for one day. My word, what a shock those men must have had, when they saw us all crawling out from their own private entrance ! "

CHAPTER 19

AN EXCITING FINISH!

UNCLE BOB went down the hill at a quick pace, followed by the four jubilant children. Punch hopped along behind on three legs, his left hind one still very bruised and painful. Nicky turned round to make sure that he was following, and gave a sudden loud exclamation.

" Look! Look what Punch is carrying! "

They all turned—and how they laughed! Punch carried a shoe in his mouth—rather a large one—with a bite right through the leather!

" It's the shoe belonging to Harry, the man that Punch bit! " said Nicky. " Dear old Punch—you *had* to do your shoe-trick didn't you—and bring a shoe along somehow? Drop it! "

" No," said Uncle Bob. " It might be useful. Let him carry it. Which man did it belong to? "

" Er—well, I'm afraid you'll think it's queer—but actually it belonged to a one-eyed man called Harry," said Ken. " The man whose name we put at the end of our secret message."

" How extraordinary! " said Uncle Bob. " I'm

beginning to think that you and Nicky must be in league with this band of thieves—how else can you possibly know so much about them ? "

Everyone laughed. Nicky turned to his uncle. " I say—we never came up at night to listen to the nightingales," he said. " What about it, Uncle ? We might find something else peculiar to look into. I can hear a bird singing now—and I'm sure it's carolling something about a golden statue ! "

" Ass ! " said Uncle Bob. " But my word— that statue really is a marvellous find, you know. There'll probably be a fine reward for that—and you kids will get it ! "

This was a most exciting thought ! But there wasn't much time to consider it for they were now down in the town. Uncle Bob walked straight to the police station and asked for the superintendent. The children went with him, feeling VERY important.

The superintendent listened in amazement, for he knew Uncle Bob and his work very well. He took rapid notes, telephoned sharply to somebody, called in three of his men, and rapped out some orders.

The children listened in excitement, but couldn't quite understand what was happening. The super-intendent turned to them at last, and smiled.

" You've done some very good work ! " he said.

" I congratulate you. We shall have to ask you to identify these men for us, I'm afraid, once we've caught them, but we will let you know when that happens."

" Yes, sir," said Nicky, thrilled. " And, er—what about the golden statue, sir ? "

" Well—we'll see to that at once," said the superintendent, smiling. " I doubt if it's *gold*! I can't say I've ever heard of it myself. But there may be many other quite valuable things in those old cellars—or caves, whatever they are ! There must be *something*—or those men wouldn't have gone to so much trouble, digging under the hill. It's likely that the big bearded man you heard called Hassan is the one who knew about the cellars and what they might contain—he may even be a descendant of the family of the prince who built the old mansion up on Skylark Hill."

" He ought to have kissed the feet of the statue and wished for success," said Winnie. " Then he might have got everything he wanted ! Only, of course, he wasn't lucky enough to *find* the statue ! "

The superintendent laughed. " Did any of *you* kiss the statue's feet and wish ? " he asked.

" NO ! " said Nicky. " We're not so silly. But wait a bit—one of us *did* ! "

" Who ? " said the other three children, in astonishment.

" *Punch* did—I saw him licking the feet ! " said Nicky. " That's his way of kissing. Punch—what did you wish for ? "

" WUFF ! " said Punch, at once.

" He says he wished for an enormous, meaty bone," said Nicky, in such a serious voice that the others all laughed. " All right, Punch—your wish will soon come true—granted by the magic power of the Golden Statue ! We'll buy you a bone on the way home ! "

" WUFF ! " said Punch again, delighted.

" Well—I think that's about all for the moment," said the superintendent, smiling. " We'll let you know when we need you again—and that will be when we've rounded up the men."

" Look—Punch is still carrying that shoe he brought from the caves," said Ken, when they were outside the police station. " Uncle Bob—ought we to leave it with the police ? "

" Well—let him take it home, and we'll wait till they ask us to go to the police station again," said Uncle Bob. " I don't expect it will be long before we get a call to go. I feel that the superintendent had a very good idea where to look for those men.

Uncle Bob was right. The police went at once to the next town where they had reason to believe that a small colony of foreigners had made their headquarters a few weeks back. They looked for the men that Nicky and the others had described to them.

But no—not one of the men seemed to resemble the children's descriptions! There was no man with a long dark beard, no man with a dark shade over one eye—and all of them denied knowing anything at all about the old burnt mansion, or the caves in the hillside.

" Well—you will please come along with us for an hour or two, for questioning," said the police officer, and hustled the men into the police van. A car was at once sent to the children's homes, with a message for them to go to the police station, and Uncle Bob, too. They piled into the car in great excitement. Punch went with them, of course!

The men were paraded in front of the four children. But what a disappointment! Not one of them seemed to be like the men they had seen underground—or those the girls had met coming down the hill! Not one had a beard—or wore an eye-shade.

But Punch recognised them! He growled and showed his teeth. He strained at the lead and tried to get at one of the scowling men.

" Sir ! " cried Nicky to the superintendent, " I believe that man is the one called Harry that kicked Punch and hurt him. He must have taken off the black eye-shade we saw him wearing.

Punch bit right through his shoe, sir, and made his foot bleed—and he even carried home the shoe ! The man couldn't wear it, because his bitten foot was bleeding and hurt him. We've brought the shoe with us—just in case it might be useful. Here it is ! " And Nicky promptly placed it on the superintendent's table.

The superintendent snapped out a few words, and the man sullenly took off his right shoe and sock. The foot was red and swollen, and teeth-marks could be plainly seen. Punch gave a blood-curdling growl, and the man edged away, scared.

" Put this other shoe on — the one the boy brought," ordered the superintendent. " See if it fits."

It did, of course, though the man pretended that he could not get it on !

" It's the same type of shoe that he's wearing now, sir," reported the sergeant who had been watching. " A foreign type, sir. Must be his ! "

The man mumbled something angrily, and put on his other shoe again, easing it on gradually because the bite that Punch had given him was still painful. Nicky noticed that his hands were shaking.

One of his friends noticed this too, and took out a packet of cigarettes. He offered it to the big man, who took one thankfully. He was obviously in a state of panic.

Nicky stared at the cigarette packet, and so did Ken. It seemed somehow very familiar! Ken gave a sudden shout.

" *He's* one of the men too, sir—the one with the cigarettes."

" How do you know? " asked the superintendent, astonished.

" Well, look sir—the cigarettes are called Splendour Cigarettes—and we found an empty packet up in that old mansion! "

" Ah ! " said the superintendent. " Got the empty packet with you? "

" Yes, sir," said Nicky, and took out the packet from his pocket. " AND we found an empty match box, sir—and these dead matches. Quick-Lite matches they're called. I kept them in case they were clues ! "

" Well, well, WELL ! " said the superintendent, surprised, and he took them from Nicky. " Search the pockets of these men, Sergeant, please."

The men stood sullenly while their pockets were turned out. Aha ! Two of them had " Splendour " cigarette packets, and one had a box of " Quick-Lite " matches.

" There you are ! " cried Nicky, thrilled. " This is the gang all right, sir. They were probably the signallers up in the tower—they smoked cigarettes and threw down the matches, and the empty box

and packet. And the shoe belongs to *that* fellow—
he's called Harry. And I'm sure that the biggest
fellow is called Hassan. He has shaved off the
black beard he wore ! "

" You know, my boy, you should be of quite
considerable help to your uncle, when you're a
little older," said the superintendent, smiling
broadly. " Take the men away, Sergeant. I'll
deal with them later."

Uncle Bob, the children, and Punch went out
feeling very jubilant. Uncle Bob stopped outside
a shop.

" I think," he said, " that we should all go in
here and celebrate the triumphs of that fine bunch
of detectives, Nicky, Ken, Winnie and Penny—to
say nothing of that remarkable sleuth, Punch, who
knew when to turn a most annoying shoe-fetching
trick into a wonderful CLUE. Punch—will you
kindly lead the way ? There cannot be another
dog in the world who can catch a criminal by the
simple method of stealing his shoe ! "

Everyone laughed. They trooped into the shop,
which sold the biggest and creamiest ice creams in
the town. Uncle Bob promptly ordered two each.

" What—two for the dog as well ? " said the
shopgirl in amazement.

" Certainly ! And bring six bottles of ginger-
beer," said Uncle Bob.

" Ginger-beer for the *dog*, too ? " said the shop-girl, quite dazed.

"Why not ? " said Uncle Bob. "He likes ginger-beer so why shouldn't he share in our celebrations ? Don't you agree, children ? "

"Oh, YES ! " said everyone, delighted that their little dog should be honoured. Punch barked joyfully, and ran round giving everyone a loving lick. He had quite forgotten his bad leg.

The ice creams were delicious. The ginger-beer fizzed and bubbled in the glasses. Uncle Bob raised his glass and spoke solemnly, with a twinkle in his eye.

" Here's to the ' Mystery-That-Never-Was,' which turned into the ' Mystery-That-Came-True ' ! " My congratulations to you all—and apologies for disbelieving you. And let's hope the Golden Statue brings you the good luck you all deserve ! "

" Hear, hear ! " said everyone. And Punch joined in too. " Wuff-wuff-wuff-wuff ! " What a time he had had ! *What* an adventure !

" All the same," said Ken, solemnly, " it's the very last time I'll *ever* invent a mystery. Honestly —I never *guessed* it would all come true ! I'll be jolly careful in future, and so will Nicky ! "

No—don't be careful, Ken ! Invent another one, and do tell us what happens then !

THE ENID BLYTON TRUST
FOR CHILDREN

We hope you have enjoyed the adventures of the children in this book. Please think for a moment about those children who are too ill to do the exciting things you and your friends do.

Help them by sending a donation, large or small, to the ENID BLYTON TRUST FOR CHILDREN. The Trust will use all your gifts to help children who are sick or handicapped and need to be made happy and comfortable.

Please send your postal orders or cheques to:

> The Enid Blyton Trust For Children,
> Lee House,
> London Wall,
> London EC2Y 5AS.

Thank you very much for your help.

Nightmares

Bloodcurdling tales of gruesome terror!

Edited by Mary Danby

DON'T READ THIS BOOK…

If you're afraid of rats and spiders…. If you can't stand the sight of blood…. If you won't go to sleep with the wardrobe door open….

But if you're made of sterner stuff, dare yourself to try these fiendish horror tales — every one a nightmare of shuddersome fun!

Armada

THE
WHIZZKID'S
HANDBOOKS

1, 2 & 3

Peter Eldin

Is the strain of school giving you brain failure? Don't despair — there *is* a cure!

These hilarious Handbooks will tell you all you need to know to become your class Whizzkid and always Come Out On Top. Each book is packed with jokes, puzzles, brainteasers and tricks — plus a delicious bunch of devilish devices to make and stunts to pull. There are lots of useful hints and tips, too, to help you baffle your teachers with your brilliance.

Stop Press

Now there's a *third* book in the series. At last — the complete survival kit for every schoolkid!

TOP SECRET
ADULTS
KEEP OUT!

Armada

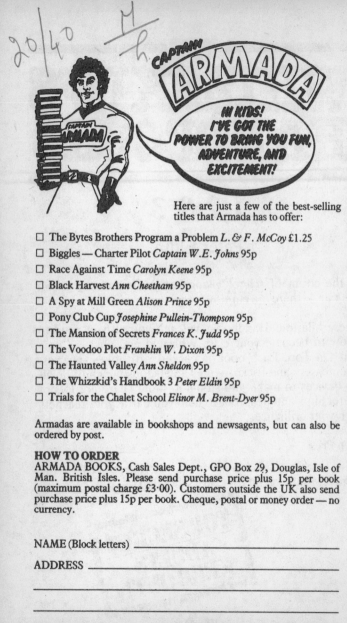

CAPTAIN ARMADA

HI KIDS! I'VE GOT THE POWER TO BRING YOU FUN, ADVENTURE, AND EXCITEMENT!

Here are just a few of the best-selling titles that Armada has to offer:

☐ The Bytes Brothers Program a Problem *L. & F. McCoy* £1.25

☐ Biggles — Charter Pilot *Captain W.E. Johns* 95p

☐ Race Against Time *Carolyn Keene* 95p

☐ Black Harvest *Ann Cheetham* 95p

☐ A Spy at Mill Green *Alison Prince* 95p

☐ Pony Club Cup *Josephine Pullein-Thompson* 95p

☐ The Mansion of Secrets *Frances K. Judd* 95p

☐ The Voodoo Plot *Franklin W. Dixon* 95p

☐ The Haunted Valley *Ann Sheldon* 95p

☐ The Whizzkid's Handbook 3 *Peter Eldin* 95p

☐ Trials for the Chalet School *Elinor M. Brent-Dyer* 95p

Armadas are available in bookshops and newsagents, but can also be ordered by post.

HOW TO ORDER
ARMADA BOOKS, Cash Sales Dept., GPO Box 29, Douglas, Isle of Man. British Isles. Please send purchase price plus 15p per book (maximum postal charge £3·00). Customers outside the UK also send purchase price plus 15p per book. Cheque, postal or money order — no currency.

NAME (Block letters) _____

ADDRESS _____

_____

_____